A Dream of Light

Sara Jo Easton

D1445599

To anyone who feels they don't fit in.
Know that you have friends.

That cliff looks high enough to spot things, said a voice that was strangely within Eramine's head as the words were spoken. Eramine instinctively ducked down further, and when she looked to True for guidance, True had her eyes closed as if in a deep and urgent prayer.

At the very least, it is land, another voice echoed. *We must get our bearings. Without the stars for guidance, we have little help. It is too bad Lord Idenno's spirit doesn't speak to us.*

It has been almost two weeks, the first voice said with anxious urgency. *We must find this Eramine before it is too late.*

True whimpered before covering her mouth.

Eramine, on the other hand, blinked in surprise that she was the topic of conversation. When she felt a few earth-shaking thuds, it was sheer self-preservation that kept her rooted to her spot rather than running out to demand answers.

We will find her, the second voice said, and the daffodil green monster stepped forward. *I know we will.*

I could accept no less, the blue monster was now in Eramine's field of vision, and the monster's grey eyes were narrowed as if in genuine worry. *Cully-*

Cully wouldn't want you to feel this way, the green monster lifted her tail and gently touched her companion's side.

Cully would have been out here himself, and he would have found our savior Eramine sooner, the blue monster sighed and turned her head in precisely the wrong direction. *But it seems we have company.*

True screamed and turned her bow toward the monsters, aiming an arrow and firing directly at the blue monster's side.

Eramine drew an arrow and prepared to do the same, until she saw the fear in the other monster's golden eyes as True's arrow met its mark.

Ouch! The blue monster winced, and turned to glare at True. *I can assure you, though we may look terrifying, that was unnecessary. We mean you no harm.*

I can even help you, the golden-eyed monster added as she examined the arrow. Then, to Eramine's shock, the monster simply lifted her tail, knocked the arrow out and instantly healed the open wound with a simple touch from her suddenly-glowing tail.

"Help us?" True shouted. "Your kind has done nothing but kill us!"

Kill you? The blue monster frowned and shared a knowing look with her companion. *I can assure you, that is the furthest idea from our minds.*

We need your help, the other monster said. *Do you know an Eramine?*

"No," True said, a little too quickly to sound truthful. Then again, this was the first time to Eramine's knowledge that anyone had heard True tell a falsehood. It was pretty much the reason she earned her name in the first place.

What about you, child? The blue monster asked gently, though there was that urgency back in her tone that told Eramine a wrong answer would make the monsters travel further inland, where the village was.

That could never happen. If all those stories about her parents' deaths were real, sending the monsters to the village would result in countless deaths.

"If I did, why is Eramine so important to you?" Eramine didn't lower her bow, but she did tilt her head to study the monsters' reactions.

If we don't find her, the Heir of Senbralni will die, and Eramine might die as well.

True shrieked and started openly weeping.

"Why are two lives tied to finding one person?" Eramine asked loudly, praying that the monsters didn't notice True's blunder. If they did, they they would know to keep searching the immediate area and the village until they found Eramine.

Because the child has stated, in no uncertain terms, that Eramine is to be her Bond, the golden-eyed monster said. *To Onizards like us, to be a Bond is a sacred and rare honor. It involves permanently linking your mind with another's mind, to the point where your pain is their pain. We Bond at birth, if we choose that path, and if a Bonded child were to not find their Bond...*

I cannot think of that, the blue Onizard said shortly as she turned to True. *Are you Eramine? You look like my brother's Bond, Zarder Jena.*

"Jena?" True turned pale, as if she had been stung by a blast of ice.

Please, if you are Eramine, we would do anything to help you, the golden-eyed Onizard said. *If you come with us, you would be practically royalty.*

For what it's worth, the blue Onizard mumbled.

"I would rather be a beggar than a royal slave!" True screamed, doing nothing to correct their false assumptions about her identity.

There are no slaves in the Sandleyr, the blue Onizard seemed puzzled, almost offended. Surely she realized what her vast size conveyed to humans?

If anything, we are your slaves, for we made a vow to protect you, the golden-eyed Onizard said. Then, after a moment's pause, she added, *My name is Senquena. I am a healer, in case you couldn't tell.*

11

And I am Rulraeno, the blue Onizard said proudly. *I bring the good will of the two kingdoms and the three zarders.*

"That sounds...pompous," Eramine said, though she winced as the Onizards turned their attention back to her.

I agree, Rulraeno said. *Those are not my words, but I believe my mother and my nephew wanted to impress Eramine with her future role as Bond to the Heir of Senbralni.*

"The what to the who?" Eramine's whole face contorted in confusion, especially since every mention of this Senbral thing seemed to make True sink lower in fear.

Too many words, Rulraeno. Your brother had the right approach, Senquena sighed as she turned back to True. *Eramine, you must know that an innocent child dying, and needs your help. We can explain the rest later, but you have a zarder's heart. To abandon a child is not in your nature, I know it.*

"One less of you seems a better bargain to me," True said harshly.

You do not understand the situation you find yourself in, Rulraeno said. *One less child is also one less of you.*

"Are you threatening me?" True drew another arrow and aimed for Rulraeno's throat.

No, we want no violence! Senquena shrieked and stepped between Rulraeno and True. *Please do not aim your weapons. We are here to serve and protect you.*

"You can protect me by leaving this place!" True shouted.

I suspect we were mistaken, Rulraeno said pragmatically. *Eramine is not here. I suppose we should go and leave these poor humans alone. Perhaps*

12

that village we saw west of here is where Eramine lives.

Eramine thought of the village elders' reaction to the two Onizards, knowing now that their kind was probably responsible for the massacre that happened when she was a baby. Arrows would fly, and no doubt the Onizards would strike back. No matter what, there would be bloodshed, and she suspected Senquena was going to be the one to shed it if someone tried to harm Rulraeno. There was no choice. She had to protect her people.

"I am Eramine!" she shouted, to the apparent surprise of everyone. When she felt the stares of the Onizards upon her, she put her bow back onto her shoulder and added, "I will go where you will take me, if you will leave my people in peace."

"Era, no!" True screamed. "You don't understand what these monsters plan to do!"

"I understand these Onizards do not wish to harm us," Eramine said in an echo of their previous words. "I also hope that they will bother us no more if I go with them."

You have my word, on my brother's star, that we will not harm you, and we will leave your people alone if you ask it of us, Rulraeno said with a flourish of her wings and a formal bow.

Eramine was not certain how anyone could own a star, but the vow sounded heartfelt and genuine. "Swear to me also that you will let me return if I ask of it."

"Era, don't make this sacrifice!" True sobbed. "Your brother-"

"Marinel isn't here, and he would do the same thing to protect us if he had to do so," Eramine said.

13

I don't think you understand how much power you will have being the Bond of this particular child, Senquena said. *She is related to-*

"Swear to me!" Eramine shouted as she picked up her bow again. "I don't care if she is the heiress of the night itself! I will return safely to my brother when this is over."

Rulraeno frowned and stared for a long moment, as if she was pondering what to reveal. *I swear we will help you return to your family when this is over. But there is no time to lose. We can take both of you if we need to, but Eramine must be back at the Sandleyr for the hatching.*

"True will stay," Eramine said, before leaping onto Senquena's tail. She didn't like the idea of abandoning her family, but Eramine wasn't certain True would ever recognize the necessity of her choice. As she scrambled up the Onizard's back, she shouted, "Go now, before I change my mind!"

"Eramine!" True's screams echoed across the cliffs as the two Onizards took off. A few arrows flew into the air, but clearly these Onizards were skilled at flight, for they dodged the arrows as if they were nuisance flies.

Eramine's last thought before they entered the storm was that her dream of flight was not at all like she planned.

Chapter 2

Marinel was filled with a sense of unease that couldn't be explained away by merely the storm in front of them. As a matter of fact, while the storm looked treacherous, it was not as rough around his ship. Even if it were to suddenly take a turn for the worse, he had weathered many similar calamities with the help of his crew. While potentially dangerous, the weather couldn't explain Marinel's growing concern.

His dread also couldn't be explained away by the ring buttoned in his front pocket that he had purchased for True on the voyage. That decision was the easiest he'd ever have to make, for she was the only person he loved more than his own family, and the only woman he'd ever have eyes for.

All things considered, his life was going well indeed, which was why Marinel was suspicious. Nothing had come easy for his people in ages, yet suddenly everything was relatively calm. It was as if the waves crashing upon his people were receding, only to build up into a great tsunami upon the proverbial shores. During this latest voyage, every one of his usual trading stops held rumors of strange creatures landing in villages seeking a human child, then apologizing and leaving when everyone rightly denied any knowledge of human children. That was why they were returning home early now; his village had few children, but one of them was his sister.

"Captain!" Jamarius, the ship's helmsman, shouted over the wind as he held a tight grip over the wheel. His sienna skin was covered in sweat from the effort of keeping the ship on course. "I can see the shore, but there is a black flag of mourning on the cliffs!"

Marinel ran to where his best friend was standing to get a better view. A black flag of mourning meant that extreme danger had recently befallen the village, and that the ship had to remain cautious upon arrival. Sure enough, instead of the light woods of the ladder they'd fashioned for those on watch for the village, a large cloth with the rarest, darkest dye they'd been able to purchase waved pitifully with the wind. But if the ladder wasn't visible, that meant someone was still on the cliffs, hidden from view. There was no way to cut the ladder down from the bottom of the cliff, and it would not be lifted up out of view unless someone was purposefully taking a defensive position.

"Whose turn was it on watch?" Marinel asked hopefully. Whoever was on watch would be safely ensconsed on the cliff face, hidden from every danger. It was one of the many reasons he made sure his sister was put on watch duty as often as possible.

"True, I think," Jamarius said. "If not, I doubt anyone or anything would be dumb enough to cross her. She's got the best aim and the swiftest feet, and I'm sure she's looking after little Eramine."

16

"True can take care of herself quite well," Marinel admitted with no small swell of pride. "It's the others, such as the elders, that I worry about."

"They can take care of themselves better than you'd think, Captian," Jamarius said. "They survived the attack all those years ago, after all."

"You shouldn't speak of such a bad omen," Marinel shuddered. "Hasana, do you see anyone hiding in the rocks?"

"Of course not!" called the young woman sitting in the crow's nest. Her brown skin had a strong bronze undertone from the previous sunny days they'd experienced. "If I did, they wouldn't be hiding well enough to protect themselves from arrows!"

"Sound the horn," Marinel commanded. "I want everyone to know that we're home, and if there is someone still out there waiting to harm us, they will know we aren't afraid of them."

Hasana played a few low notes on the horn she kept with her at all times, and the ladder dropped down the cliff face.

"She's still there," Marinel said, "She hid under the flag! Quick, get us to the cove!"

The crew worked as a team to turn the sails in just the right direction to catch the winds to the cove near the cliffs. Marinel normally watched to make sure no one slipped in their duties, but his eyes were on the copper-haired woman who was climbing down the ladder tenuously. There was so much risk when wet wood met unsure feet, and True was not climbing as carefully as she normally did. Indeed, by the time she was on firm earth, her knees gave out from under her and she collapsed.

"True!" Marinel shouted, jumping into the water and swimming the remaining few yards rather than waiting for the ladders and anchor to safely drop.

He had been gone too long, and he couldn't bear to think of what could have happened to the woman he loved while he was away.

"Marinel!" she called back, her voice tinged with the hint of heavy crying. "Marinel, I failed to protect her."

There was only one 'her' that he and True ever talked about, for they had acted as Eramine's surrogate parents ever since the calamity at his sister's birth.

"True," Marinel said softly as he reached her and sunk down to the earth to hug her. "Where is my sister?"

True didn't seem to have the heart to tell the answer, for she wordlessly clung to Marinel as she sobbed.

"True, I know you did what you could," Marinel hugged her close as he bit his lip to hold back the emotions that were running through his head. "Tell me what happened, and we'll fix this together."

This declaration made her slowly raise her eyes to his. "The monsters came for her."

"No," Marinel gasped as his shoulders sank and tears came to his eyes. "No, it can't be...we sailed as far away as we could from where we last saw them."

True sank down with him. "I tried to stop them, but there were two of them this time, and one of them is able to heal things instantly. They told her some lie about a dying child, and she went with them after they threatened to go to the village to look for her."

"Oh, my brave Eramine," Marinel cried for an unchartable amount of time while True held onto him. Then, when it seemed he had spent as many tears as he possibly could, he said, "We have to save her. I will get the ship ready."

18

"Are you insane?" Jamarius shouted, the first alert to Marinel that his crew had made it to shore. "She just said there are two monsters, and one of them can heal instantly! What chance do we have against that? We barely survived the attack when we were children!"

Marinel took a deep breath. "I will not ask anyone to go with me. If I have to take a small fishing boat and leave my father's ship behind, I will do what it takes to save my sister. It is what I would hope any of us would do for anyone of our village. Yet I know I am asking a lot of someone to take the journey with me, and I will not mandate anyone to go on this voyage. If you are willing, come help me prepare. It may be my last journey, but if I could choose a final journey I would gladly choose one of love for my family."

"Then take me with you," True said as she checked to ensure her bow was properly around her shoulder. "If it is to be your last journey, I would rather be by your side than anywhere else in the world. Besides, I couldn't save Eramine. I will carry that guilt with me for as long as I live."

"True, I love you," Marinel held her hand. "I hold you blameless, but I would be glad to have you with me."

"You've got me with you as well," Hasana set her horn on her shoulder and stepped forward. "You're going to need a lookout, and I can't trust anyone else to do my job."

"I will go with you as well," True's father said as he stepped forward slowly. His skin was pale and wrinkled with age, but his voice was as strong as the muscles he'd earned by being one of the members of Marinel's crew. "Long ago, I lost my first wife and daughter to one of those monsters. If it hadn't been for your father finding me wandering aimlessly on the shore in grief, I would have died from my burns. Then, just as I felt a tiny bit of happiness in my life again, the monster stole True's mother from me as well. I will never forgive them for what they have done."

"We will bring justice for them, or die trying," True hugged her father tightly.

A few more members of the crew stepped forward and volunteered, all of them offering personal stories of loss and strength. Marinel was overwhelmed by the amount of people willing to save his sister.

"Well, if you all are going on this crazy mission, I will help you," Jamarius said. "I just wish there was another way. I'm the last one left out of all my family, and I'd like to carry on our name someday."

"I have no choice," Marinel said firmly. "You will understand that one day when you have a new family of your own."

"That seems to be a rather gargantuan 'if' right now rather than a 'when'," Jamarius shrugged. "But I will go. Someone has to help you keep on the right course, and you need all the friends you can get."

"Marinel," True's father said softly as he put his hand on Marinel's shoulder. "You should do what you originally sailed out to do. You have my blessing."

Marinel shook his head. "It would be a bad omen when this day has brought us so much grief."

"It is a bad omen to leave on a journey with nothing but sadness, and it would give us all hope where none existed previously," True's father folded his arms.

"Arvid," Marinel sighed. "She deserves better than this."

"What are you talking about?" True frowned and gripped Marinel's hand tighter.

20

"My True deserves to be more than the girl who waited for her turn for someone to stand up for her," Arvid said firmly. "Besides, there are few rooms on the ship, and I am certain she'd rather share space with you than with her dear old dad. You know my rule about you two sharing a room. Not before the hand-binding ceremony."

Marinel smirked. "Well, when you put it like that, I suppose you are right."

"I am right here, you know," True said. "You two don't have to talk over me and speak in vague terms as if I were a child. Why are you talking about the hand-binding ceremony?"

Marinel grinned and wiped at his eyes before he reached to his pocket, grateful the ring had remained buttoned into place. "True, we're trying to avoid spoiling the surprise, but I suppose there's no avoiding that now."

True gasped as he held out the ring, a simple band with a fire opal in the center that matched the copper in her hair.

"True, will you marry me?"

"Yes!" True started crying again, but this time there was a bit more joy in her expression as he slid the ring onto her finger. "We always swore we'd cross oceans for one another."

Marinel frowned. "I had hoped that didn't involve sailing towards monsters and possible disaster."

"Nevertheless, we will face any challenge together," True said. "And I swear to you, I will slay the monsters and save your sister as a wedding present."

Chapter 3

Taking the girl with us without her saying goodbye to her people is going to haunt us, Rulraeno.

Rulraeno sighed and turned to her side, where young Eramine was safely riding in the space between Senquena's neck and wings. The child looked happier in the air than she did on the ground, but Senquena looked as if they had violated a sacred law. Rulraeno feared that she would never meet Senquena's expectations for her, mostly due to the fact that she didn't understand them. Given this mystery, she hoped that Senquena hadn't noticed the fear Rulraeno had felt when she thought that the copper-haired human was going to harm them. Rulraeno wasn't necessarily afraid of death, merely the death of someone close to her heart.

It is done, and I will be the one who answers to how it was done, Rulraeno said privately. Then, to bring the conversation back to their charge, she added, *I hope you will grow to be our friend over the time we spend together. We have been searching for you for weeks now, and I can't tell you how happy we are that we have found you.*

Onizards don't wed, we become joinmates, Senquena said lightly.

"Oh," Eramine said, "Well, when did that happen between the two of you? It's clear from the way you act with each other that it is going to happen, if it hasn't already."

Curse it, Senquena was blushing at the very idea of it. Rulraeno hadn't even officially outed herself to her parents yet, and here was a human girl already guessing Rulraeno's feelings.

Well, she was going to have to put a stop to the speculation for now. *Let it be perfectly clear,* Rulraeno said as she stood tall and proud. *Senquena is my friend. I would do nothing to hurt a friend or endanger the friendship.*

***

As they landed on the island's sandy beach, Eramine slid down Senquena's tail before she looked carefully at the two Onizards. She noted that Senquena had not lifted her eyes since Rulraeno had been "perfectly clear", and there was an odd new red tone to the Child of Earth's cheeks. Eramine also noted that Rulraeno, for all her boldness, seemed disheartened afer her explanation.

"I see," Eramine said. "I didn't mean to offend. I won't bring it up between the two of you again."

Thank you, Senquena said softly. *Now, I will find us food and shelter, if you don't mind.*

"Why would we mind that?"

Senquena shrugged, then turned and started running across the nearby field.

27

Rulraeno sighed. *Senquena hates discussions about her romantic attachments, or lack thereof. To be fair, it embarrasses me as well, so I understand her concerns.*

"If there is nothing between the two of you, and you are merely friends, why is it an embarrassing subject?" Eramine asked. "For that matter, even if there was something between the two of you, there would be no shame in that. What is really wrong?"

Rulraeno frowned. *Quena was bullied in the past when rumor had it she had feelings for a young and stupidly cruel Child of Water. I don't believe she actually did have feelings the way the rumormongers made it out to be, but the damage was done.*

"Bullied...for feelings?" Eramine frowned. The idea made less sense than the idea of a Child of Water, whatever that was.

I agree, it is stupid. My mother tries to fight it, but some Onizards still act like they're living under the Fire Queen, when feelings could get you hurt or killed.

"I really don't like hearing about this Fire Queen," Eramine said.

Luckily, she is long gone from this world. Leyrkan Senraeni in his youth defeated her, and Lady Amblomni ended things once and for all. They are the heroes of the Sandleyr, and you are lucky that your Bond is going to be part of their noble tradition of Onizards Bonding humans.

The way Rulraeno suddenly folded her wings and bowed her head told Eramine that there was more

Chapter 4

The cavern was large enough to fit the entire village into it, but it made Rulraeno and Senquena appear comically large. The two Onizards spent an awkward amount of time getting their wings situated in such a way that they weren't touching the archways of the cave or each other. Eramine would have laughed if she hadn't heard Rulraeno's confession earlier. Now it seemed only the awkward discomfort of someone who was too afraid to tell the simple truth and take a risk that their wings would touch on purpose.

Senquena, if she knew of the situation, seemed more concentrated on the fire Eramine was creating than anything else. *I always wished that I knew how to do something like that,* she said. *It's not a particularly useful skill when a Child of Fire could simply breathe it to life, but to create a fire of my own would be nice.*

"I would think healing people instantly would be more useful," Eramine said as she coaxed the embers to life.

Oh, it isn't always instant, but I will always heal without question or prejudices, as per the Code of Earth that guides me, Senquena said. *But I have always felt that one shouldn't be tied to serve only one purpose. With that in mind, I learned how to tell this story from my great-grandmother, and I tell it each time a new child is born to explain our world to them.*

Eramine added the few pieces of driftwood she had found while searching the island, and made certain that firelight was dancing throughout the cave. "I would love to hear it."

Senquena nodded, and both Onizards bowed their heads, as if they were in prayer. Eramine guessed they couldn't be worshiping the same deity as her people, but she still recognized the solemnity of the moment and remained quiet. Then, out of the silence, Senquena began to speak:

When the world was young, there was no light, for the Great Lord of the Sky who created this world could see all creatures without it, and they were equal in His eyes. He made the Children of Water, guardians of the sea and the rivers. To keep the world from getting cold, He created the Children of Fire. To keep the world dancing, He created the Children of Wind from the first of the storms. To keep the others strong, He created the healers, the Children of Earth. Finally, to keep us grounded, He created the humans.

Without the light, we did not recognize our purposes, and any outsider was treated with distrust, Senquena shuddered. *No one knows how many lives were senselessly lost, how many dying creatures the Children of Earth failed to heal. What we do know is that the Children of Water and the Children of Fire were at war with one another over some senseless nothing long lost to history.*

Senbralfi was a Child of Fire, and he was bent on vengeance when he snuck into the land of the Children of Water. He found a young woman, wandering alone, and saw it as his chance to kill for the first time and prove his worth.

36

monster came to destroy them. Maybe unnamed love was the greatest love of all.

They had no name for what they felt, Senquena said, *but that did not make it less of an emotion for it. Senbralfi did what he could to hide Maerno's existence from his kin, but there came a day when his people discovered the homes of the Children of Water.*

Rulraeno bowed her head at some unseen horror.

Senquena, too, seemed disturbed by the idea of this event she had never witnessed, for she remained silent for a moment before she explained, *the Children of Fire were prepared to kill everyone who wasn't a flame-breather. Senbralfi tried to stop the senseless violence, to tell everyone that they were the same, in spite of different powers. But he could not stop the blasts of fire from destroying the feeble structures the Children of Water had constructed for protection. The battle was a bitter one, for their powers were evenly matched, and each side was easily capable of killing the other.*

Maerno lost Senbralni in the battle, and as she screamed his name, her voice made her a target for both sides. The Children of Fire found her first.

"No!" Eramine screamed.

Yes, Senquena said. *Yet in the end, it was not Maerno who felt the flames hit her body, but her beloved Senbralfi. He had jumped in front of the blast to shield her, and had paid for it with his life.*

"I'm not sure I like this story," Eramine said.

It seemed that he was dead, Senquena said as she held out her tail as if to caution for patience. *Yet the Great Lord of the Sky had been watching the battle with disgust, and He knew that He would have to bring light into the world if the violence was ever to end. So He gave the light to Senbralfi, who transformed before*

39

an astonished Maerno into what we now call a *Child of Light*. *His skin was as radiant as the sun he would one day become, and everyone but Maerno trembled in fear of him. Senbralni, as the Great Lord of the Sky now called him, was made undisputed Leyrkan of the united Onizards.*

No one deserves that much power, though, not even someone who first brought love and light into the world, Senquena said. *So he was gifted the power of empathy; he could feel how others felt around him, and could even sense the pain of death if he was close enough to a dying creature.*

Eramine thought about this for a moment. "So if he ever tried to be a tyrant, the pain of everyone would be his pain as well?"

Precisely, Senquena smiled. *Senbralni in his wisdom established a united home of the Onizards out of the ashes of the homes of the Children of Water. To ensure everyone lived a healthy life for as long as possible, he made the Children of Earth swear the Code of Earth we still follow today, to heal without question or prejudices. Then, to ensure that no one forgot their similarities, he gave just enough of his powers of light to some Onizards so that they would be able feel the emotions of one other and also be mentally Bonded to that other.*

"So that's why you keep talking about Bonding!" Eramine laughed. "It makes a little bit more sense now. But what happened to Maerno? It seems like she got the poor end of the bargain, for she got no powers of light, even though she loved just as much!"

Rulraeno grinned. *Ah, this is my favorite part of the story. Maerno and Senbralni dwelled together in harmony for years, and they raised four children together; their descendants still dwell in the Sandleyr today. When it was finally time for Maerno and*

40

Senbralni to die, the Great Lord of the Sky made Senbralni the sun, but He made Maerno the rest of the sky, so that she would not be thought of as lesser for the entire time they were together.

Eramine smiled as she thought of just how wide the sky was in comparison to the tiny sun. "So she protects him, as he protected her."

Exactly, Senquena said.

"Then it is as my people say about our ancestors," Eramine said. "Until we learned integrity, loyalty, and heart, we were nothing, but when we gained it, we gained everything."

Chapter 5

Marinel listened to the gentle rock of the ship as he held his sleeping bride in his arms. Though the storm was occasionally making its presense known with flashes of lightning and the fall of rain against the deck above them, the seas seemed relatively calm. Too calm, in fact, as if they were in the center of a hurricane. It was enough to make him concerned, even with the knowledge that Jamarius was steering the ship with just as much care and dexterity as always. Perhaps it was paranoia, but he had too many people depending on him to dismiss a concern without checking on it.

Marinel kissed True's forehead and moved his arms out from underneath her.

"Mmhm," True mumbled and reached out to touch his shoulder. "Do you have to leave?"

"I'm still the captain while we're on the seas," Marinel sighed. "I will be back to you as soon as I can."

"Don't dawdle, sailor man," True said. "I'll save a spot in the bed for you, but I can't promise I'll share the covers if you take too long."

Marinel laughed as he put on his pants. "Well, plenty of married life ahead of us to sort that out."

True smiled. "Married life. I like the sound of that."

"Me too," Marinel said. "So with that in mind, I need to check on everything to preserve our lives."

With one final shared kiss, Marinel left his quarters and climbed the short ladder leading up to the deck of the ship. For not the first time in his life, he was grateful that the ship was small enough to view both the helm and the stern from the center of the ship. There were ominous clouds all around them, but where they were sitting the rain was calm, and the seas calmer. The wind was even gentle against the sails, giving just enough to propel them in the right direction without endangering anyone who might be aboard.

"Strange weather, Captain," Jamarius called from the wheel. " It's not a hurricane; when we sail further, the clouds are parting for us as if guiding the way. If all storms could be like this, I'd be greatful. Your True is a good omen."

"Well, my father did name this vessel the *True Sails* before True earned her name," Marinel said as he finished his climb and walked to the back of the deck where Jamarius stood. "Seems only fitting she'd be good luck whenever she's aboard."

"I just hope we're equally lucky when we catch up to the monsters," Jamarius said. "I hope you have a plan other than sailing out in the open and challenging them."

"I do," Marinel said. "They're sailing due north by True's description. If they follow that path, they'll reach Arrow Island by next nightfall."

"That's dangerous indeed," Jamarius frowned. "Did Eramine have her pouch with her when she got carried away?"

"True said she still has her bow and arrows, and her pouch," Marinel said. "Meaning she has the antidote for the freezeneedle poison. As long as she has that, we'll be able to forge the properly strong arrows to slay the monsters once and for all."

"It'll take days to prepare enough, I'm guessing," Jamarius shook his head. "It's a good thing we have the antidote on board as well. I don't rightly like the idea of firing that stuff toward Eramine."

"It's better than what we had," Marinel said. "And it's certainly a better plan than nothing."

"Well, True is the best shot we have," Jamarius said. "I'll steer us toward Arrow Island as long as I know that she's going to be the one aiming her bow."

"I'll only trust True and a few other capable people with this task," Marinel agreed.

"Good," Jamarius said. "Now get back to your wife. It isn't right to be leaving her in the middle of your wedding night to listen to your friend complain about business."

Marinel nodded and laughed, before turning toward the ladder where his True awaited him. He paused only a moment, when a wisp of a strange blue form appeared on the horizon, floating around as if in the middle of a dance. Marinel blinked and the form was gone, so he uneasily convinced himself that he had imagined it and went back below deck.

Chapter 6

I am a Child of Earth, and this is my Code.

Eramine sat upright and glanced around the cave, noting that her fire had been extinguished and that the two Onizards had left the cave. Theoretically, if she found a way to sneak away, she could escape and get back to her people.

Then again, if she did escape for now, there was no stopping the Onizards from chasing after her again. As the only one of her kind around, Eramine was at a distinct disadvantage in size, strength, and agility. It had already been proven that the Onizards were not intimidated by arrows, so her bow was useless at the moment. Plus, she had no idea where she was or where she would be able to construct a ship to get home.

Putting thoughts of escape away for the moment, Eramine noted that Senquena was standing at the entrance of the cave, staring at the ocean in the distance as she repeated a strange series of sentences over and over again.

I will heal without question or prejudices, giving preference to those who have the worst wounds. I will not put myself above others, for my life is the

Sandleyr, and the Sandleyr is my life. I am a Child of Earth, and this is my Code.

"How long did it take you to memorize that?" Eramine asked as she stepped toward the cave entrance.

Senquena blinked a few times as if coming out of a trance. *Oh, good morning. We have been waiting on you. You had a confusing day yesterday, and we knew you needed rest.*

"So that thing you were reciting, is it some sort of tradition like the other stuff you were telling me about?"

Indeed it is, Senquena smiled. *When I developed my powers, I memorized the Code of Earth to remind myself to stay on the right path through life. It is so easy to be selfish or prejudiced, and so hard to put others above yourself. But when you do, there is a chance that you can be someone's hero, and what nobler goal is there?*

"I don't know," Eramine frowned. "I'm not sure what being a hero means anyway. Why is it so important to you?"

Heroes get to live a life respected by others, Senquena said. *Heroes can sometimes even have a chance to be happy.*

"And you aren't happy now?" Eramine frowned some more. "You should be able to be happy without heroic deeds or recognition from others. Why can't you be happy just being yourself?"

Myself has need for improvement, Senquena said. *I find that by pushing myself toward a heroic ideal, I can find happiness even if I don't achieve the heroic ideal. Perhaps that is why I was destined from birth to be a Child of Earth.*

"I don't know, it sounds lonely," Eramine said.

46

Not as lonely as Rulraeno's life, Senquena said as her gaze turned toward the ocean.

Eramine rubbed her eyes a few times to confirm the strange sight in front of her; the giant Child of Water was drifting and diving in the waves, and swimming as if she belonged there more than on land or in the sky! She was using her wings as a sail when she was above water and as fins when she dived below water.

"I should have guessed that would be one of her powers," Eramine sighed. Well, her plans of building a ship after escaping were gone. Clearly Rulraeno could be a treacherous leviathan if she wanted to be one.

It isn't a power, Senquena said. *She is the only Child of Water who has learned to do that. She does that whenever she starts thinking about her brother Delculble or Delculble's Bond Ransenna. They were her friends as she grew up, and now they are dead through association to her family.*

"What?" Eramine gasped. "But how and why?"

A monstrous Onizard woman abandoned the Code of Earth and killed multiple Onizards just so she could be the lead healer for the Night Kingdom, Senquena folded her wings tightly against her chest and bowed her head. *She broke the Code of Earth and put herself above others, and Rulraeno paid the price for it. Rulraeno's closest sibling and his Bond are dead now, and she is still mourning years later. I wish I knew how to break her out of her shell.*

Eramine debated telling Senquena what Rulraeno had confessed, but quickly decided against it. There was no way she needed to get involved in the business of the feelings of superpowered monsters.

"Doesn't she have other family members or friends that she can talk to about this?" Eramine asked.

No, Rulraeno said as she emerged from the water, her focus in their direction for the first time. She seemed tired and resigned as she stepped back on shore. *My mother is Leyrque, one brother is Leyrkan, my other remaining brother is grieving the loss of his joinmate, and my sister is the definition of perky happiness that I don't want to destroy. You know, I can hear you when I am in the water.*

Oh, Senquena said softly. *Well, I hope I didn't reveal anything that offended you.*

No, she deserves to know why I will sometimes require time alone on this journey, Rulraeno said. *Also, why this child she is supposed to Bond is so important to me; the child is Delculble's grandchild, and since he only had one son, this child and his or her sibling is the last remaining link to him. I couldn't save Delculble, but I can save the child.*

"Why didn't you just tell me that instead of that nonsense about the ancient bloodline?" Eramine threw her hands up in the air in exasperation. "That is a goal that makes a lot more sense. I know I would do anything to protect my family."

Children of Earth aren't the only ones who put others above themselves, Rulraeno lowered her tail. *We've dawdled too long here; I don't want us to be late to the hatching.*

Eramine stepped back onto Rulraeno's tail and climbed up her back, but there were too many new questions she didn't have the answer for.

Chapter 7

Marinel woke to the sound of True cleaning the room, and the sight of her efficiently organizing his paperwork as if she had always been there brought a smile to his face. Then, reality hit him as he remembered the reason why she was sailing with him in the first place.

"Jamarius says we're sailing to Arrow Island," True frowned as she looked over the shipment paperwork for the last voyage. "I don't like this idea of putting Eramine at risk, even if she can take care of herself. I am afraid; what if my arrows miss their target?"

"That will never happen," Marinel laughed as he slipped out of bed and stepped over to stand behind his wife. "Your arrows never miss."

"I missed when I tried to stop the monsters when they took her," True sighed and leaned against him.

"If you had succeeded then, she would have fallen into the water and died. You won't miss when the time is right," Marinel said as he wrapped his arms around her.

True reached up and held his hand, and they stood together looking over the navigational charts. "Once we get past the Isle of Graves, we'll be sailing into uncharted territory. I hope we're making notes; we could probably sell an accurate map to other traders if we survive this."

"We can have a section that says 'Here there be dragons' and it will be literal," Marinel smirked.

"That was a terrible joke," True grinned.

"Well, these are terrible circumstances," Marinel said. "If we can't have terrible jokes to go with them, what are we?"

"Fuddyduddies," True said. "I can't have that."

"Nor I," Marinel hugged her and kissed her neck. "So I take it you talked to Jamarius while I was asleep?"

"Just returning the favor," True said. "He also said that he's willing to manage the ship while we catch up on some rest."

"Oh did he?" Marinel raised an eyebrow as he spun his wife around to face him. "And do you intend to take advantage of the helmsman's generousity, my darling?"

"I do," True kissed him. "The way ahead is dark, and I would forget it for a while."

"Then let's get the rest we are going to need," Marinel smiled as he navigated his wife back to the bed and slipped back under the covers.

Chapter 8

Eramine...

It felt wrong to wake up in a place without light or definition. How was it she was hearing a voice that was so clear, yet so distant at the same time? Why couldn't she see anything? The only time she had felt this way in the past was the strange dreams with the wings.

"This must be a dream then," Eramine frowned. The wrongness of knowledge about the dream should have been enough to jolt her awake, but instead the mysterious voice was seemingly holding her in place.

Eramine, the woman's voice rang out again. *I apologize for intruding. May I show myself?*

"It would be less creepy," she said. "Who are you?"

A golden Onizard with grey eyes like Rulraeno's slowly appeared before her. *I am not a fan of this method of communication, but I have no other way to talk to you yet. My old friend once insisted that I should ask permission before using my powers to enter other people's dreams, and he had the right idea. Still, I agree that a voice without a form is, as you say, creepy.* The golden Onizard smiled. *My name is Rulsaesan, dear. It is a pleasure to meet you.*

"So you're the Leyrque," Eramine frowned. "They didn't tell me you had freaky dream powers. Am I supposed to bow, or what?"

I am the Leyrque, but please don't bow. You are a future zarder, which these days has more weight, it seems. Rulsaesan smiled.

"What is a zarder, anyway?" Eramine asked. "They said it a few times, but they never explained it at all."

Goodness, how silly, Rulsaesan laughed. *A zarder is a human Bonded to an Onizard.*

"Oh," Eramine stared up at Rulsaesan. "That explains it. But there are only three zarders?"

It'll be four when your Bond hatches, Rulsaesan nodded. *Mind you, that's not from lack of human ability, but rather lack of opportunity.*

"Ok," Eramine smiled and nodded, not really wanting to know why her species' ability was mentioned as if it were originally questioned. "Why are you in my dream anyway?"

I am here to meet you and to check in on my daughter.

"Rulraeno seems...bitter," Eramine said, for lack of a better word. "She has been doing her best to be kind, but she is so reserved and focused on her mission that she declined to talk things over with my people before we left."

Rulsaesan cringed. *Your family must be worried.*

"I think my brother might try to sail after me," Eramine said. "I think I saw the sails of his ship when we were travelling today, but I might have just imagined it."

Rulsaesan sighed and bowed her head. *My daughter is so focused on proving herself that she misses the bigger picture. I had hoped Senquena would balance that out.*

"Senquena seems too busy reciting the Code of Earth over and over again," Eramine shook her head. "I've heard it so many times now that I could recite it from memory, and I don't even have the cool healing powers that are supposed to come with it."

Rulsaesan sighed again. *We have our work cut out for us. Senquena may be focusing too much on the part of the code that puts others above herself. She needs to reach out for what she wants if she is going to find the happiness she is looking for.*

"We?" Eramine folded her arms. "What am I supposed to do about it?"

Their heads are in the clouds about their mission, Rulsaesan said. *I suppose that is my fault; I sent them out together and implied they were the only hope of you reaching the Sandleyr in time. Yet I suspect that is not the case; your mind is strong, and things have a way of working out the way they should.*

"Are you saying I alone can bring them down to earth?"

No, Rulsaesan said. *That would be insane. I'm just asking you to help them remain focused on each other. Don't let them lose heart, and above all stay safe.*

"You do realize that everyone else needs to stay safe from them, right? They are bigger than the tallest ship!"

You underestimate your own kind, Rulsaesan said. *A single human brought down a tyrant, restored the Night Kingdom, and inspired my people to enter a new age of enlightenment.*

"That's a bit much to ask of me," Eramine said. "I'm fourteen years old and I've never been away from home."

53

Well, no time like the present, Rulsaesan said. *I have found that most people have more heart than they give themselves credit for if they only take the time to let it shine out.*

"So how do I do that?" Eramine asked.

Rulsaesan smiled. *You will know when the time is right. For now, it is time for you to wake up.*

Chapter 9

How is it this child can fall asleep on my back like this? Rulraeno asked. *I'm flying on prayers to the Sky Lord that she doesn't fall off.*

We aren't far from land, Senquena shrugged and stared at the shoreline in the distance. *It has a decent beach, at least, but it doesn't look like there are any caves or other landmarks to hide behind.*

Fair enough, as long as we can switch her over to your back for a while, Rulraeno said.

"I'm not going to fall asleep again," Eramine yawned and stretched her arms. "Rulsaesan had me under some weird dream spell to talk to me."

Oh, I hate those powers! Rulraeno smiled for the first time in ages, and Senquena noted that it looked good on her. *She used to talk to me like that when I was in hiding as a child. She always spoke some vague platitude and then woke me up when I started asking too many questions!*

"Yes, exactly!" Eramine laughed. "It's like she wanted to get involved, but she didn't want to tell me how she wanted me to get involved. Does she really talk like that with everyone?"

I don't know, Rulraeno said as she landed on the shore. *I haven't bothered asking, and it hasn't seemed worth getting worked up over.*

Senquena couldn't help but be thrilled that Rulraeno and Eramine seemed to be finding common ground. Perhaps, with time, they could even be friends. Senquena's delight was shortlived, however, when she took a look at the ground around them.

Rulrae, don't move, Senquena hissed. *Don't look, and don't move.*

You said don't look, and of course that was the first thing I did, Rulraeno gasped and shuddered as she saw hundreds of plants with sharp, spiked needles. *Deypin.*

Don't worry, you didn't land on it, Senquena said more lightly than she felt. *You just need to step backwards; it isn't behind you on the beach, just in front of you. You're going to be fine.*

We should have brought a Child of Fire with us, Rulraeno shuddered. *I thought we wiped this stuff out of existence!*

"You can't wipe that out, it's a weed," Eramine said as she leaned over Rulraeno's shoulders and stared at the plants. "Sure, it's harmful if you get stabbed enough times, but if you have the antidote it shouldn't be a problem."

Antidote? Rulraeno gasped and trembled.

There is no antidote for deypin, Senquena frowned and stared at the child. *Our healers have searched for it for ages to no avail.*

"They must not have looked very hard, because the antidote is everywhere too," Eramine reached into the pouch she was carrying and held out a strange looking plant Senquena had never seen before.

There is no antidote for deypin, Rulraeno said as her voice cracked ever so slightly. *There can't be.*

"Sure there can be," Eramine said, though her voice sounded less confident. "Actually, it's good that we found this stuff, because I need it if I'm going to hunt for food later."

You hunt...with deypin poison? Rulraeno said, her claws digging into the ground immediately in front of her. Luckily, even in her tension she controlled herself enough to avoid the needles.

"It's more humane than just firing an arrow at something and waiting for it to bleed out," Eramine said as she slid down Rulraeno's tail, seemingly oblivious to the Child of Water's distress. "With the freezeneedle plant whatever gets hit just gets paralysed and can't feel the arrow."

No, you have no idea what it feels like, Rulraeno growled as she stepped back toward the open ocean.

She doesn't know what happened, Rulrae, Senquena tried to warn.

Well, she should know then, Rulraeno said. *Whatever you hit didn't feel the arrow, because every drop of blood in their body gets stuck in their lungs. It is not a painless death; they can't move, they can't breathe, and they feel like they are drowning until their lungs finally give out and their brain shuts down. The entire time, they are scared, in pain, and wishing for an end to their suffering. Your people are monsters if you use that stuff.*

"We give enough of the cure that the creature doesn't feel anything," Eramine said. "I suppose your kind has a gentler way of killing what you eat."

We eat plants! Rulraeno shouted and backed further into the water. *Even if we didn't, that stuff is the last thing I would ever use. I wouldn't wish it on my worst enemy.* With a final sob, Rulraeno ducked underneath a wave and swam away.

Wait! Senquena shouted. *If we explain, I'm sure she will help us destroy it.*

Rulraeno flicked her tail at the surface and dove underwater.

Eramine stared off at the waves, then looked carefully at the plant in her hand. "I didn't mean to offend her."

You couldn't have known, dear, Senquena sighed. *Like many, Rulraeno has wounds that are not at the surface for all to see. There are many Onizard families that have been harmed by this stuff you're calling freezeneedle.*

"I don't understand. I would have thought a powerful race like you guys would have known how to stop the poison. How could you guys survive on plants and not know about the salveweed plant?"

I can assure you, nothing like that stuff grows around the Sandleyr, Senquena said. *If it did...stars, we could have saved so many lives with it!*

Eramine stared out into the water, where Rulraeno was angrily splashing around. "Including her brother's life?"

Senquena sighed. *Her brother got the worst of it, for he wasn't even the one stabbed by the stuff. His Bond was the target, for she was the adoptive mother of the Heir of Senbralni. Delculble felt everything that she just described through his link to his Bond, and he died from his mind being broken on his Bond's death.*

"This Bonding stuff is sounding more and more dangerous," Eramine said. "If I am to be a part of it, what am I to gain from it?"

You'll gain a best friend, and an ally who knows how you think, who will look out for you when no one else will.

"I don't know," Eramine looked around before drawing something in the sand. "I already have that in my brother and with True."

Is True the woman who was pretending to be you to protect you?

Eramine nodded as tears came to her eyes. "I know I hurt her by telling her to stay behind, but if both of us were gone, my brother would have no one and no explanation as to why."

I don't like how we left, Senquena said. *I am positive it will haunt us later. Still, we will make sure you are treated like the royalty you are destined to be.*

"I don't want to be royalty," Eramine said firmly as she sketched more things into sand. "I just want to be myself."

Perhaps you can be both, Senquena said as she watched Rulraeno gliding through the waves.

Chapter 10

"They were here, Captain!" Hasana shouted with delight. "There are tracks in the sand, and Eramine wrote us a message!"

Marinel ran over to the side of the ship to get a closer look and smiled when he saw the writing was still fresh.

"We are close," he said, before turning to shout to Jamarius. "Well done!"

"Just following orders, Captain!" he chimed back.

"What does the message say?" True called out to Hasana as she walked over to Marinel's side.

Hasana's head darted back and forth over the writing for a moment before she said, "I have the salveweed. They don't know what salveweed is. Freezeneedle kills th-argh, a monster footprint cut off the last of it."

"There are tracks backing away from it all the way to the water," Jamarius said. "Underneath, the tracks aren't as measured. It's a good thing we got here before the tide washed these clues away."

"Freezeneedle kills them, that's clear enough," True said as her eyes lit up. "Marinel, this plan could work. We might have a chance."

Marinel nodded as grim thoughts of a final confrontation filled his head. "Gather every needle you can find, Hasana, and get the crew to join you. Do it quickly, so we can keep our advantage. Jamarius, you should go to your quarters to sleep. I'll take the helm for the rest of the day so that you have a chance to rest, then you can take the night's watch so I can spend time with my wife."

"Any orders for me, Captain?" True asked.

"I can't order you around, dear, and you know it," Marinel laughed. "But if you can help make the arrows, I would be grateful."

"I'd only trust my own arrows anyway," True said. "Praise be that we have a stronger chance to save her than we did yesterday."

"Praise be," Marinel agreed as he stared out at the open ocean and the raincloud in the distance.

Chapter 11

Hey Eramine, come join me in the dream!

Eramine opened her eyes and found herself on the cliffs again, with the grey-winged creature from her original dreams floating in front of her. The creature didn't have the same command of her form that Rulsaesan had, however, and it presented an odd effect of random body parts appearing only to disappear a second later.

Sorry, I can't really tell what I fully look like yet, the childlike voice chimed. *You must be getting closer, though, 'cause I had an easier time of finding you.*

"Who are you, and why have you been showing up in my dreams?"

I'm going to be your Bond! The child spun around. *I'm going to hatch soon, so I hope you'll get here in time. I'm looking forward to properly meeting you.*

"I don't understand this Bonding stuff, anyway," Eramine said. "All I've been told is that it makes me a princess and that if I don't do it, I'll die."

The child wrinkled the bit of her nose that was visible. *Grownups are dumb sometimes. I don't want to be your Bond because of death if we don't, I want to be your Bond because you are smart, and brave, and you love your family! I want to be all of those things, and I know that I'm going to need help when I get older. The grownups say if I hatch before my sister, I'm destined to rule the Night Kingdom as the Heir of Senbralni. Doesn't it sound just a little bit...pompous? It scares me.*

Eramine was alarmed at having her own word thrown back at her, in the same type of discussion. "Are you reading my mind right now?"

No, but our minds are similar. We have the same characteristics and values; it's the only way the Bonding could ever work. Great Uncle Senraeni is a quiet, contemplative, brave Onizard, so his Bond is quiet, contemplative and brave. Cousin Xolt is rash and silly sometimes, but he cares deeply about his family, so he was lucky to find a Bond who was all those things as well.

"How do you know all of this if you haven't hatched yet?"

My Mom and Dad tell me stories of how I came to be. The child smiled. *At least, I know what they'd tell a baby, so we have a lot of love from family, but I can't tell exactly what happened in the past to make the grownups all...weird. Whenever certain things come up, they seem like they're going to cry.*

"I don't know everything, either, and it's frustrating," Eramine said. "I do know that an Onizard killed my parents and half my village when I was born. I know that Rulraeno is grieving her brother's death, but Senquena seems like she's just above it all with full knowledge of everything and no intention of doing anything about it!"

The child shook her head. *That isn't what's happening at all. Senquena is grieving too, just in a different way. To take on the quest to find you would have required bravery as well as a desire to prove something. That's what Mom keeps telling Dad. She seems to be convinced that Rulraeno and Senquena have to work together, and those two specifically!*

"Rulraeno told me she had feelings for Senquena," Eramine said cautiously. Technically, it was betraying a trust, but for goodness sake if she couldn't talk about whatever she wanted in her own dreams, what good were dreams for?

Oh, okay! The child giggled. *We're matchmakers, then! This could be fun!*

"This doesn't add up. First Rulsaesan, then your mom is suggesting matchmaking. I get that matchmaking is a nice thing to do, but why on earth would matchmaking be considered on equal par with making sure we survive this Bonding thing?"

I dunno, but it can't be that difficult. They're united toward a common goal and they are in close contact with one another. Plus, we know at least one of them likes the other. How tough can it be?

Eramine pondered Senquena's aloof, self-hating nature and Rulraeno's grumpy swim sessions. "If you met them, you might think differently."

The child grinned mischieviously and disappeared.

"Wait, no!" Eramine called out, "That would be a terrible idea!"

There was nothing but the sound of the waves hitting the cliff, though, and with that Eramine woke up.

Chapter 12

Senquena opened her eyes in a state of utter confusion. She took a moment to confirm that she was no longer dreaming, and found herself grateful that she was back on the island and not seeing weird images of pieces of Onizard children giggling and teasing her. Yawning, she took a look at her surroundings and noted that Rulraeno and Eramine were already outside talking.

"Again, I'm sorry I gave her the idea," Eramine said. "She's rather strong-willed. I will say, it was nice to have a normal conversation with her rather than hearing her creepily call out my name and disappear. I guess she's getting stronger."

It doesn't make any sense, Rulraeno said. *That power has always been reserved for Children of Light. If the child is capable of using those powers already, it means that one of the four Children of Light is feeling weak and sick, possibly near death. But they were all healthy when we left the Sandleyr.*

You had a weird dream, too? Senquena asked as she stepped out of the cave they had found for the evening.

"Yes," Eramine said. "I talked to my future Bond, and she got the idea to try talking to you two."

The little girl kept giggling and telling me that I needed to spend more time with Rulraeno, Senquena fought the blush that she knew was coming to her face. Rulraeno, after all, had already made her position on the matter clear, and there was no need to complicate things. *I finally forced her to go away when I thought up a dream without her in it.*

What they didn't need to know was that the dream she had envisioned involved Rulraeno slowly stepping out of the water and smiling as she walked over to Senquena's side and whispered a pet name for her…among other things.

Rulraeno's color was redder now as well; stars, what was in her dream?

The child thought it would be a good idea to try to bring us closer together, to help us on our quest to get Eramine back to the Sandleyr, Rulraeno said. *I told her that the journey back would have to be easier than the journey to find her, but the child just laughed and reminded me that we'd already nearly pierced ourselves with deypin, and Eramine's brother and sister-in-law are apparently also following us.*

"I knew it!" Eramine exclaimed. "Wait, how did she know that? And what do you mean, my sister-in-law? My brother isn't married."

Rulraeno frowned. *That status has apparently changed within the last three days. At least, it has changed according to the child, but she doesn't know everything. The last bits of the dream she tried to show me were not something that could come true.*

"They got married without me?" Eramine sat down in the sand. "Why would they do that?"

They think they are going to die saving you, Rulraeno said as she folded her wings against her side.

66

What would give them that idea? Senquena shuddered. *We made it perfectly clear we wished no one any harm.*

"True has always taught me that words and actions are two different things," Eramine said as she stared off at the horizon. "True and Marinel always told me that there was a creature, like you guys, who breathed fire and torched our village the day I was born. Something that happened that day has to have convinced them that your words mean nothing."

I would give anything to understand what happened, Senquena said softly.

Chapter 13

Marinel opened his eyes to a wall of flames and the sound of screams. A hand grabbed his and pulled him from his tiny bed just in time to avoid the beams of the roof falling on top of him. Marinel blinked his eyes a few times, trying to push away the nightmare that he knew was coming next.

"Run! Guard your mother!" his father shouted as he pushed Marinel toward the field of flowers his family was growing for trade. In the distance, he could see the rest of the village aflame, along with all of the food crops. He could also hear unearthly laughter, but his mother gave him no time to see anything but the flowers, and in the distance, the wild and untamed sea grass that glowed the color of copper in what sunlight was still visible.

"Marinel," his mother collapsed to the ground, clutching her stomach. "Run, I will meet you later."

"No, Mama!" Marinel knelt down and held her hand. "You need help!"

"Heed your mama," True's mother, her brown skin covered in ash, seemed to appear as if by magic, but she was likely running behind them the whole time.

"No!" Marinel snapped. "I'm going to be a big brother! You need me to help you! I'm going to help!"

"Shush!" True's mother pulled both him and his mother toward the sea grass. "Do you want the fire monster to hear us?"

Marinel shook his head, unaware that fire monsters existed but certain he didn't want to meet one.

"Then help me help your mama."

"The baby's going to come," Marinel's mother winced and pushed herself forward as she spoke.

"I know, we're here for you," True's mother said. "Let's just get you as far away as we can."

Silence during birth, even in dangerous circumstances, is not possible for a baby, and Marinel's sister was no exception. True's mother had no sooner handed the baby to Marinel before loud footsteps thundered behind them.

Fascinating, the monster said as she focused her blood red, angry eyes on the bundle in Marinel's arms. *Is that a brand new human?*

"Yes," True's mother shuddered. "Leave her in peace, please. She has not had a chance to live yet."

Perfect, the monster turned her head, revealing a hideous scar under her eye that made her look even more intimidating. *Just what I need. Name it Erstai and I will let it live as my personal aide. It will be above all humans when it helps me raise up the next Heir of Senbralni.*

"Era...mine," Marine's mother gasped.

Oh, I would be cautious, the monster said. *It would be the aide of royalty instead of a pile of ash, which is more than a human deserves. Just give it to me.*

"Her name is Era...mine!" Marinel's mother somehow managed to shout loud and clear in spite of obvious weakness.

A wall of flame engulfed both mothers, and Marinel screamed over and over again to try to wake himself up and out of seeing it again. But it was no use; no matter what, the flames would never go away, much like the scar within his soul.

The baby crying caused the monster to wrinkle its nose in disgust. *Stars, tell it to pull itself together!*

"Babies cry when they are born; no one can stop them from doing it," Marinel's younger self trembled as he debated whether or not to use his back as a shield. Perhaps if she breathed flame on him directly instead of on the grass around them, he could keep his sister from being overtaken by flames.

Ugh, useless, the monster scowled. *It is too dumb to understand then. My valuable time is wasted.*

"Wait!" Marinel kneeled before the monster before she had a chance to breathe death again. "Babies cry when they are born because they learn how helpless they are. But she can learn to serve you."

How? The monster squinted as if she were trying to wrap her mind around a problem.

"I will teach her to obey," Marinel said. "I will teach her to be strong, and I will teach her to serve."

How can I trust you? Humans lie.

"If she is not to your liking, we would both die," Marinel closed his eyes to hide his fear of the monster's gaze. "I know you could kill me now, so I have no reason to lie."

Imminent death is the best reason to lie, the monster said. *Yet the hope of a slave who is raised to know her place intrigues me enough to let you live for*

70

now. My future child will be the Heir of Senbralni; once I persuade the father to remember his place, I will need help to care for our child. I will need the most obedient servant.

"She will be one," Marinel said in a voice firmer than he felt. "The remaining humans in my village will see to that."

You grow bold, the monster frowned.

"No," Marinel said. "Just set on your task. The more who can instill fear of you in her, the more she will know how bad an idea it is to fail you."

Very well, they can live, too, the monster said. *I have had my sport anyway. As fun as this was, I suspect the only real joy I will have is putting my man in his place.*

With that cryptic remark, the monster flew away, leaving Marinel to cry along with his baby sister.

"Are you mad?" True screamed as she ran out from the sea grass. "You promised her away, when our parents fought for her freedom! How dare you…" True couldn't finish the sentence without sobbing over what was left of her mother.

"I promised she would obey," Marinel said. "Eramine will obey us. I promised Eramine will be strong, and she will be strong enough to kill the monster. I also promised Eramine will serve, and she is going to serve her people like her mama and her daddy before her. I never promised her to that…that creature."

True's expression softened slightly. "What if we are the only ones of our people left?"

Her words echoed as he awakened, and for the first time he thought he heard the strange echo of a woman crying as well.

71

Chapter 14

Things are much worse than I thought, Rulsaesan said as she stood in Eramine's dream fighting back tears. *Did you know your brother risked his life to save you the day that you were born?*

"Yes," Eramine said cautiously. "True told me that story all the time. She said he loves me more than life itself. I always thought she was exaggerating, like family normally does when they talk about love for one another."

I intended to enter his dream as a diplomatic mission, but I saw his nightmare instead, Rulsaesan said. *It is nightmare that we partially share, I have discovered. We had the same enemy, and the same fear; the Fire Queen, bent on destruction, determined to kill. I learned she killed your people just for a chance to find you and mold you into a perfect slave for the Heir of Senbralni.*

"That title keeps coming up," Eramine said. "I don't like it very much, and I'm positive my Bond doesn't like it either."

Of course not, Rulsaesan said. *It seems to be a curse. But I stupidly told my daughter to mention that title as something to be proud of your Bond wielding. The Fire Queen specifically mentioned the title Heir of Senbralni by name after she murdered your parents.*

"No," Eramine gasped.

I should have remembered how much of a curse that title really is, Rulsaesan sighed. *We meant to tell of your importance to us, of how well we would treat you when you arrive at the Sandleyr, and instead...*

"My brother thinks I'm being taken to the monster that killed our parents, to possibly be tortured or even killed," Eramine frowned. "True will probably be preparing freezeneedle arrows."

Freezeneedle?

"Your kind calls it deypin," Eramine said. "I have the antidote, and before I knew the full picture about what's going on, I wrote a note in the sand that I had the antidote."

Stars, Rulsaesan cursed. *They will not discriminate in their use of these arrows?*

"True trained herself to be the best shot our village has ever seen after her mother died," Eramine sighed. "She will fire towards me if she thinks I will be able to give myself the antidote safely."

They probably think your death would be a better fate than serving that monster, Rulsaesan sobbed. *I can't blame them; the world was instantly made better the moment she died. I saw the scene of your parents dying once, but the stars know how many times your brother has seen it in his nightmares.*

"He never once complained about nightmares," Eramine frowned.

I doubt he would complain about anything to you, Rulsaesan said. *Siblings protect one another.*

"There has to be a way to prove you mean us no harm," Eramine threw her arms up into the air. "A good fourth of your kind are healers!"

Many sacrifices have been made to get you to this point, Rulsaesan said. *I fear a great sacrifice will*

73

have to be made to make the two sides reconcile. I pray it will not result in another death while I am Leyrque.

"True is probably the best archer the world has ever seen," Eramine snapped. "Someone is going to get hurt if we don't do something to stop the confusion!"

Then we can be the cure, the faded form of Eramine's Bond-to-be appeared, and Rulsaesan jumped back.

What are you doing? Rulsaesan yelled. *You shouldn't be here! Your mother must be worried sick. You could be making her sick!*

I'm more natural in Eramine's mind than you are, the future hatchling scoffed. *And yes, she is worried sick. That's why I'm here; I want to make her happy by making everyone else happy!*

Listen, Rulsaesan's voice was firm, and the expectation of obedience rang with every syllable. *Your mother loves you very much. She loves you more than she loves your father, and she challenged the Fire Queen to a fight to the death to rescue him. Eramine is almost there, and your time will come.*

Are you? The child's voice rang out with hope as she turned to Eramine.

"I am," Eramine smiled bravely. "And the next night when we meet, I'm sure we can meet my brother and convince him that we are safe, if you are willing to try with me."

The child seemed to take this sentence for the hidden meaning it contained, and squealed with delight. *They're coming, Ibral!* she shouted before disappearing the way she came.

Rulsaesan frowned. *Well, now I know your future Bond's name before you do, which is highly against tradition.*

"Your traditions have Senquena praying every morning and night by reciting the Code of Earth. Maybe some traditions need to change."

Praying? Rulsaesan shook her head and paced around a few times. *That isn't a tradition. That is a rather alarming compulsion.*

"Oh," Eramine frowned. "Then why-"

That is something only Senquena can answer, Rulsaesan said. *Listen, it is more important than ever that she and Rulraeno are one team.*

"They already are," Eramine laughed. "They are working toward getting me to the Sandleyr in time for the hatching."

I think you know better than to presume that is what I meant, Rulsaesan said. *But this dream journeying is weakening me, and I must leave you for now. Take care of them, please.*

Chapter 15

Senquena awakened to the feel of water beneath her legs and the the sound of Rulraeno shuddering at the mouth of the random cave they had found for the night. There was a brief moment of concern before she located Eramine sitting on a rock shelf above her. Then, she simply took the time to enjoy the feel of the water against her skin.

High tide must have come in, Senquena mumbled as she stretched her legs.

The water was rising, Rulraeno took a deep breath. *I was afraid we would have to flee.*

Senquena squinted. *But you swim every day.*

Not in a cave, Rulraeno muttered. *There's too much that can go wrong. I don't know why you insist on hiding in them.*

"If everything is going as I expect it is, my people are building deypin laced arrows in a misguided attempt to save me," Eramine said. "I think the caves are a good idea."

Well I...do not, Rulraeno shrugged lamely. *These places, they aren't like the underground leyrs of the Sandleyr, which was formed by the teamwork of Onizards. These were formed by the ocean itself, and the ocean will not show mercy if you get on its bad side.*

I am confident that you can protect us, should something like that happen, Senquena smiled and reached out to Rulraeno, only for her to shrug away and step closer to the part of the shoreline that had been covered by high tide.

I am not that confident, Rulraeno said. *I am sorry.*

Then, with a swish of her tail, Rulraeno dived into the water again.

Senquena sighed and folded her wings tight against her chest. *Rulrae, you could be anything you want to be and more,* she whispered. *I wish you would not give in to your fears, and would instead share them with me so we could fight them together. You blame yourself too much.*

Eramine leaned over the rock shelf and squinted at her.

I am a Child of Earth, and this is my Code, Senquena began quickly, avoiding eye contact at all cost.

"I had the most interesting conversation with Rulsaesan in my dream last night," Eramine said lightly. "She seems to think I need to push you toward a relationship with Rulraeno."

I will heal without question or prejudices, giving preference to those who have the worst wounds, Senquena stumbled slightly over the words at first, and mentally kicked herself for it. This was not the time or the place for a discussion like Eramine was proposing.

"I don't understand why, since you two have made it clear you are friends. At least, Rulraeno has said the two of you are friends."

I will not put myself above others, for my life is the Sandleyr-

77

"Is it really so bad to put yourself first for a change? It isn't healthy to live in constant servitude to everyone but yourself, you know."

- and the Sandleyr is my life. I am a Child of Earth, and this is my Code.

"Don't start the Code again, just be honest with me for a moment," Eramine said.

That would depend on the question, Senquena said as she forced herself to focus on a random stalagmite.

"Do you care for Rulraeno as more than a friend?"

Rulraeno is a wonderful woman who has many admirable qualities, Senquena said nervously as she remembered what Rulraeno had said about hearing underwater.

"That doesn't answer the question," Eramine frowned. "Would you become her joinmate if she asked?"

I am lucky to have her in my life, Senquena blinked back tears. That was a question she didn't want to ponder, for answering it was too dangerous for both of them.

"Why don't you just tell her that you care for her?" Eramine asked. "It can't go as bad as you seem to think it will."

Shall we tell her the story of how Night fell for Day? Senquena asked as her ears perked up.

Rulraeno was returning from her swim, and the moment for being asked awkward questions she couldn't answer was gone. *Really? Are we trying to depress her?*

She should know what brought her future Bond to existence, Senquena said. *Better to hear it from us than for her to ask questions of the wrong Onizard.*

Fair enough, Rulraeno said, but there was grouchiness in her tone.

There were once two Children of Fire who were the best of friends, Senquena said lightly. *Their names were Ammafi and Senmafi. The two seemed inseparable, and as they grew older they realized that they were in love with one another.*

"How sweet," Eramine smiled.

Not at all. This was terrible for Senmafi, for she was the Heir of Senbralni, and if she became the joinmate of another woman, the bloodline would die out forever. Besides, Ammafi really wanted a child of her own, and Senmafi couldn't give her one.

Eramine frowned. "But they could've-"

They formed a pact with one another, Senquena continued on, as she wasn't interested in a critical analysis of the tale. *It was a pact that they would each joinmate a critically ill Onizard for the purposes of gaining children from them, and when death freed them of their loveless joinmating, Ammafi and Senmafi could be together.*

"But those poor men," Eramine stammered. "That is cruel to use someone like that. They could have just asked for a surrogate."

It was cruel, though I don't know what you mean by surrogate, Senquena said. *Yet Senmafi's part of the plan worked as she intended. She became Senmani, Lady of the Night Kingdom, her joinmate died, and almost everyone spent the years of her reign thinking he was just a nameless nobody who abandoned his joinmate like a coward.*

"Why would they think that? You just said that he died; death isn't abandonment." Eramine wrinkled her nose from the combination of disgust and confusion.

79

Because she was a Child of Light, and Children of Light cannot survive for long without their true love, Rulraeno rolled her eyes. *Everyone assumed the best of Senmani because she was the Heir, and no one would entertain the idea that her joinmate and her true love were not the same person. Yet no one ever saw him around, so there was only one wild conclusion they drew.*

Ammafi was not so lucky, Senquena coughed, as if she were annoyed for the interruption. *Her joinmate lived, and he loved her all the more for helping him get better.*

"Oh no," Eramine whispered.

Yes, and it only got worse from there. They had a child, an intelligent child who saw there was no love between her parents. Furthermore, Ammafi became Ammasan when the Leyrkan of the Day Kingdom died, so she could no longer stay awake when Senmani was awake. She was, in a word, miserable.

"What about her joinmate?"

Ranbralfi realized his joinmate was not in love with him, so he dedicated his life to caring for his only daughter. As she grew older, he noticed she had developed a crush on Idenno, the son of Senmani. So he quickly secured an alliance by talking to Senmani's father.

"Wait, what?" Eramine frowned. "That was a terrible idea."

Lord Idenno thought the same thing, Senquena said. *He didn't know who his grandfather was suddenly insisting was his joinmate-to-be, but he knew that he wouldn't go through a loveless union like his mother did. So the unthinkable happened; the Heir of Senbralni abandoned the Night Kingdom for the Day Kingdom, where the woman he loved dwelled.*

80

"Good for him," Eramine said. "No one should be entering a life partnership with someone they don't care about. It isn't fair."

Senquena closed her eyes and sighed. *His decision would haunt both kingdoms later. Ranbralfi, when he realized his daughter was jilted, was overcome with grief, and he killed himself by throwing himself over the Sandleyr wall into the sea. His daughter lost her sanity, for she watched him fall, and she vowed revenge on those who hurt her.*

Ammasan only saw her daughter had learned to hide her emotions from Children of Light, and Ammasan did not show the care she should have shown her daughter in her daughter's time of need. Her mind was only on one Onizard; Senmani.

"But how could she ignore her daughter like that? That relationship couldn't even be possible when they ruled separate kingdoms, and children should always come first."

Senquena shrugged. *I don't know about why she ignored her daughter, especially since she was the one who wanted a child in the first place, but it is known she went into Senmani's leyr every night. They used their dream powers to talk to one another until the day Ammasan's daughter murdered them both and became the Fire Queen. Their reigns were relatively unremarkable, and their deaths in the same leyr without declaring themselves joinmates has them remembered poorly by all save their descendants.*

"This is a terrible story," Eramine said. "I am also failing to see what they have to do with anything."

Ever since that night, the people of the Sandleyr have frowned on same sex couples, Senquena said. *Once violence was committed to break up one couple, it became commonplace under the Fire Queen's rule to harm those who displayed any*

81

inclination toward caring for someone of the same gender. The Fire Queen is gone, but the fear remains. Being different is not a crime, but it is very easy for others to make you feel that it is one.

"And what was the lesson you guys took from this awful story?" Eramine frowned.

Silence is protection, Senquena said.

Protect and cherish those you care about, Rulraeno said.

"Funny, the lesson I got was not to lie and that Onizards are terrible," Eramine said. "Someone has to bring sanity and love back into the mix."

Maybe, Senquena said. *There are other things to be concerned about first, though.*

"What on earth is more important than love or sanity?"

Life, Senquena said. *And I see sails on the horizon. We should go now.*

Chapter 16

"We keep getting closer to them, only for them to fly out of reach again," Marinel stared at the monsters disappearing over the horizon as he took the ship's wheel from Jamarius.

"We have the advantage, though, Captain," Jamarius shrugged. "Their wings will tire, but our sails will keep us going as long as the wind blows strong. They will eventually have to stop for the night, but we will not."

Marinel nodded grimly. He was quite ready for this hunt to end after the last few nights of confusing dreams, most of which involved a giggling child's voice telling him not to worry, and the rest of which involved reliving the worst parts of his past. Talk about mixed messages. "How are we on arrow production?"

"If we get close enough, we have enough to fire for about a minute without running out. We should be able to up the production once we dry out the reeds we found on the last island."

"Good," Marinel said. "I want us to have every advantage we can have. The monsters have taken everything from us, and it is definitely time to take something back from them!"

A sudden rainstorm swamped the ship, and the distant creatures were hidden by the sheet of rain.

"What omen is this?" Jamarius frowned and covered his eyes with his hand. "I didn't see anything to hint at this when I was looking at the cloud cover before."

"There is definitely some sort of strange sorcery afoot," Marinel said as he caught a glimpse of light blue, transparent wings and a large tail shaped like a dolphin's fin just off the side of the ship. "Go check on True, please."

Jamarius nodded and ran below deck as quickly as he could; after all, wet wood was treacherous, and a fall now could spell disaster. Once he was below deck, the rainfall let up only around the wheel and Marinel.

The rest are all gone then, the transparent blue monster appeared on the ship, though the boards didn't creak under his weight. *Good. Let's get a measure of the man chasing after my grandchild's future Bond.*

"Who and what on earth are you?" Marinel demanded.

Wait a minute, the creature squinted and flicked his tail around. *You can see me?*

84

"Of course I can see you; if you were playing a game of hide and seek, you'd lose the moment 'it' opened his or her eyes."

You are somehow connected to my bloodline, the creature frowned. *Well then, that's all the more reason for me to find a reason to stop the fight that I see coming. It isn't going to end as you expect it to end.*

"There is only one way it can end," Marinel said. "And that is with my sister safely by my side."

You can accomplish that fairly easily without resorting to violence, the creature shrugged. *So the child is your sister, then. Perhaps that is why you can see me. But I forget my manners; I am Lord Idenno.*

Marinel reached for the bow on his back.

That would be a silly waste of resources, as I am already dead, and have been for almost fourteen years, Idenno said, before wincing. *Why'd I say that? I should have let you fire at me so that you wouldn't have anything to aim at the girls.*

"No one comes back from the dead," Marinel scoffed. "If they could, my parents would have come back to us when we needed them so many times growing up."

Idenno's wings sank to his side. *I am sure they would if they could, son. But if they are dead, know that they are stars in the night sky watching over you, and you could use them as navigational stars for your ship, I am certain. That is where all the good in the world goes when it dies.*

"So you're evil, then?" Marinel frowned.

85

No, I just made a hasty bargain with the Great Lord of the Sky when I was murdered, Idenno shifted, and part of his claws seemed to sink between the boards and below the deck. *I wanted to see my daughter grow up, and I wanted to help her be kind and to serve her people well. I was afraid, and it cost me a star. Instead, I haunt the rain, for the rain could protect my daughter.*

"Protect her from what?" Marinel shook his head and laughed bitterly. "My people didn't need to arm ourselves until your kind attacked us!"

We probably have the same fear, then, Idenno said. *A merciless, fire-breathing monster with haunting red eyes and a hideous scar.*

Marinel tilted his head in surprise. "She called herself your royalty."

It was apparently Idenno's turn to laugh bitterly. *Any royal title she had was stolen. What power she had was from her association with others. She claimed the Day Kingdom on behalf of the mother she murdered in cold blood, and when the heroic Zarder Jena and her Bond drove her out, she tried to claim the Night Kingdom through my status as the Heir of Senbralni.*

Marinel shuddered at the sound of the title. "So you're the one she planned to enslave my sister for."

No, Idenno shook his head, daring to look perplexed. *While I lived and in my afterlife, I have been an ally of humans. I died to save a human from being murdered. I helped fight to free your kind, and even in my afterlife I strive to stop all violence!*

"It's because of you my parents are dead!" Marinel screamed. "Well, you'll find that Eramine doesn't meet the specifications for meek and obedient!"

Thank the stars and the Sky Lord for that! Idenno shook his head. *I don't think you realize what she's really in for when she reaches my people.*

"She will stand up, and when the time is right we'll stop your kind once and for all!"

"Marinel, who in the furthest seas are you talking to?"

Marinel blinked to find that the creature had disappeared as True came above deck. It figured; such cowardice!

"Just testing out a speech, dear," Marinel said. "It doesn't sound quite right, though. I want to sound intimidating when we catch up to the creatures."

"You won't have to do that,"True smiled. "Just let my arrows do the talking."

Chapter 17

I tried to find him, honest, but he wasn't dreaming tonight, Eramine's future Bond pouted as she floated around the next night's dream, her wings partially unfurled. *I think he's trying to stay up late on purpose to avoid dreaming.*

"That can't be healthy," Eramine sighed. "Why would he do that, anyway? He thinks he's trying to rescue me. Shouldn't that mean he should be saving his energy?"

Maybe it isn't a choice, the future hatchling shrugged. *Maybe he is afraid for you, and his fear is keeping him awake. He does love you, after all.*

"Marinel is really good at hiding his fear; I doubt that is the full reason," Eramine folded her arms. "Besides, all those years he left me on my own with True, knowing we could be in danger at any time, he didn't seem to lose sleep."

Aww, come on, you should know better than to judge solely on how things seem, her Bond giggled.

There are layers to everything. Who knows how much worry can be hidden by determined love?

"There's so much I don't understand," Eramine said. "I want to learn."

Well, you can start by talking to Rulraeno directly, I think. She wasn't in the cave sleeping, but she wasn't in the water either.

"How can you tell?"

I asked my mama how to tell, of course, the future hatchling shrugged. *My mom is really smart, and she talks to the rain. She says the rain is my grandpa.*

Eramine would have dismissed this commentary as nonsense a few days ago, before she had seen the strange ghost in the rain. As it was now, she simply smiled and nodded. "He is, from what I understand."

Of course he is, my mama said so, the child said as if she were reciting a fact from the high deity. *Anyway, you should go talk to Rulraeno, she's sad.*

"She's always sad and grumpy," Eramine shrugged.

No, I mean really sad, the child shuddered. *Mama said if a Child of Water is surrounding themselves with water all the time, they are trying to force themselves to be happy, because they can't feel it on their own. She said if I ever need help to ask for it before I get to feeling like that. Only that doesn't make sense, because I know I won't be a Child of Water...*

Eramine frowned. "Why would surrounding themselves with water help with them feeling happy?"

I dunno, it sounds silly to me, but I know she's been swimming all the time, so she has to be really sad. Do you think that's why they want her to talk to Senquena?

"Well, Senquena is a healer," Eramine shook her head. "But no, I know Rulsaesan saw something between them. She as good as said so."

Did she really say that she knows they love each other and she wants you to help them become joinmates?

Eramine thought back to the previous dream conversation and came to a shocking conclusion. "No, she didn't, not directly. But she had to mean she wanted me to help them get together. Rulraeno already admitted she has feelings for Senquena, and Senquena has been weirdly dodging the subject by telling scary stories about the past."

Oh, about my great-grandmas? The child wrinkled her nose. *That story is sad, and it didn't make much sense. They should have just told the truth from the start and stayed together!*

"I agree," Eramine frowned. "That isn't the lesson that Senquena took from it, though."

I don't think they were listening to the same story, then, the child shook her head. *Well, you should wake up now and talk to Rulraeno some more, I think. There's a lot you and I don't understand still. There has to be a reason why they see things so differently, and even if it's silly, I want to know so I can help.*

"I agree," Eramine said. "I'm going to get to the bottom of this and do what I need to to help them."

***

Rulraeno gazed at the dark sky above her, grateful that there was no sign of rain. She didn't want any clouds obstructing her view of the stars. It had been too long since she talked to them.

Cully, her voice was like a sigh on the wind. *I know I made a promise to you, but it's so hard to keep to it. I had to step out of the cave tonight. I had to wake up, because I'm seeing her in my dreams, and I can't.*

Silence greeted her, and she expected no different. Cully's laughing voice would no longer reach her in this lifetime, and even if he were present, he wouldn't want to advise her in this matter.

Rulraeno was utterly on her own.

I miss you, Brother, she sighed and allowed herself to rest in the field around her. *I wish I had been the target instead. You deserved to see your grandchildren hatch.*

"You deserve to see your own grandchildren hatch," a voice piped up from a nearby circle of stones.

Rulraeno startled, only to see Eramine bowed over the stones, as if in silent prayer.

"I didn't mean to startle you. You seemed like you wanted to be alone, and then I saw this circle of stones, and I couldn't ignore what was written here," Eramine said softly as she traced her hands over one of the stones. It looked as if something had been carved into the stone indelicately, but with great meaning. "My brother calls this place the Isle of Graves, for it is where my parents and most of their generation are buried. I always wanted to pay my respect to them, but

91

my brother was afraid to take me. Now I know he was just trying to keep me away from the monster that looked like you guys."

Rulraeno bowed her head. *I can't believe the Fire Queen even got here. If she had touched a drop of water she would have burned her skin. Flying to a place like this, with nothing but water for miles, should have terrified her.*

"I guess she felt she had nowhere else to go, and nothing better to do," Eramine shuddered and traced her hand over the markings again. "I wish I had more stories to tell about my parents, like my brother does. At least then this pit of longing I feel when I think of them would feel less strange and awful."

I don't think grief could ever feel less strange and awful than it is, and I don't think that there's a wrong way to feel about it, as long as you don't harm others with your own grief, Rulraeno said gently. *Do those markings mean something to your people?*

"They do," Eramine nodded toward a grave that had flowers growing out of it. "That one says 'Resa, wife of Arvid, mother of Trueform.' That's True's mother. To my left, it says Bertram, husband of Maraia, father of Marinel and Eramine.' And this one in front of me reads 'Maraia, wife of Bertram, mother of Marinel and Eramine'. I added the 'Eramine' part, though the 'and' was there waiting for me to add my name like it should have been."

Your name wasn't on the grave, but your brother's was? That's rude.

92

"No, it isn't," Eramine said. "Not everyone wants to use the same name they were born with. If I won renown as a different name than what was carved here, my mother wouldn't have the honor of being acknowledged as mine."

I suppose you're right. Rulraeno said, her mind reeling. *Do your people often choose a different name than what your parents gave you?*

"Sure," Eramine laughed. "Not every name fits every person. Why would we argue if someone wants to be called something else?"

Your people are very different than mine, Rulraeno shrugged and closed her eyes as if in thought. *Anyway, what are you doing awake at this hour? Shouldn't you be resting for the next leg of the journey?*

"I'd ask you the same thing, but I heard you talking to Cully," Eramine said.

Rulraeno froze. *Well, talking to his star, really. If I was talking to Cully he'd have more to say for sure.*

"His star…is that like this stone for your people?"

Yes, Rulraeno nodded. *So you can see why swearing on his star was the highest oath I could give you.*

"It sounded like a high oath at the time, but I didn't understand the meaning," Eramine hesitated, moving her hand over a specific marking before saying, "I didn't mean to interrupt, but you were being meaner and meaner to yourself. You know, if you're feeling like you want to hurt yourself, you should talk to someone instead, even if it's Cully."

Rulraeno's eyeridge twitched involuntarily. *I will confess to having a melancholy mood more and more often on this journey, but I wouldn't do what I think you're implying. What gave you that idea?*

Eramine hesitated again. "I heard that Children of Water only surround themselves with water like you do when you swim because they are overwhelmed with sadness. There's nothing wrong with being overwhelmed with sadness, but you shouldn't keep it to yourself if it gets that bad. You should ask for help."

Rulraeno leaned her head back toward the stars and roared with laughter.

"Did I say something in the wrong way?" Eramine frowned.

No, child, you said exactly what you should if you have concerns like you did, Rulraeno said. *That said, you don't have to worry about me harming myself. My swimming doesn't have the effect that surrounding myself with rain or something of that nature would have, because the entire time I'm swimming I am also slightly terrified that I will one day do it wrong and sink to the bottom of the ocean. I don't swim to drive away the grief, because driving it away would be both impossible and dishonorable to those I grieve for. I swim because it is great exercise and it gives me time to think about what to do next.*

Eramine tilted her head. "You have been thinking an awful lot lately, then."

I have, Rulraeno turned her gaze back to the stars. *I swore to Cully and his Bond Ransenna that I'd make sure no one else got hurt, but the promise is getting harder and harder to keep.*

"You've been doing a good job so far," Eramine turned away from her parents' graves.

You are kind, but you are also wrong, Rulraeno sighed. *If I had stuck around for a while longer to explain, perhaps we wouldn't be worried about deypin arrows piercing our skin.*

"Perhaps not," Eramine looked around the circle. "But then again, it was my brother and his wife, along with the other survivors old enough to remember, who built this circle in the first place. I don't think it's easy to just cast aside the history just because someone else says they are different."

Rulraeno nodded as she stared at the stones. *We have all lost quite a bit. I am sorry I shouted at you on the island with the deypin needles. I was afraid.*

Eramine shrugged. "I understand. I just didn't know the cure wasn't around where you live."

If it was, I wouldn't be talking to Cully's star, Rulraeno sobbed as she turned her head to the dark sky above her.

Eramine held her breath for a moment. "Your grief seems like it's still fresh, but you also talk about his death like it was in the distant past."

Rulraeno smiled grimly. *It is and it isn't. Understand, when Cully died, his death was not the greatest concern on everyone's minds. The Leyrkan Mekanni had been violently murdered, and my brother*

95

Senraeni was concentrated on finding the killer. On top of that, the Fire Queen, who everyone had presumed was deceased, had just kidnapped Cully's son Iraeble.

"But every death should be the greatest concern!" Eramine shuddered. "Cully must have been worried out of his mind."

He was, especially when he found out Zarder Delma and her Bond, the future Amblomni, were chasing after the Fire Queen to rescue Iraeble. My mom tried to talk him out of wandering into the wilderness after everyone, but that was a fool's errand.

"No parent is going to sit idle when their child is in danger."

Rulraeno nodded. *What he didn't know is that while he was away, someone was poisoning his Bond. He found Zarder Delma wandering in the woods by herself and offered to take her home, but when he was flying back, he collapsed and died from sensing his Bond dying.*

Eramine frowned as if a disturbing truth was dawning on her. "Zarder Delma didn't call her Bond for help?"

Amblomni was too busy gaining her powers and finding out she was the secret Heir of Senbralni, Rulraeno rolled her eyes before she bowed her head. *Delma naturally couldn't carry Cully the rest of the way back. My brother Deldenno was joinmated to Cully's Bond, so he was in no position to help. Senraeni was trying to keep everything stable as Leyrkan, and sweet Amsaena...I couldn't let her see what I feared would be seen.*

Eramine gasped. "You mean that you…"

I tracked down his body and gave him a proper burial, Rulraeno admitted, though every word was like a weight on her wings. *So some nights his last look of terror, frozen on an unmoving face, haunts me. So I swim, and I talk to him, and I do my best to drive that image from my mind.*

Eramine stared at Rulraeno for a long moment. "That sounds like what happens to my brother and True sometimes when they think about what happened to our parents. They don't talk about it, but I can tell when the fire is on their minds. And, to be honest, it worries me, because it changes how they act, and makes them bitter."

I try my best not to be bitter, Rulraeno stared at the stars for a moment. *But my promise to keep others from getting hurt is getting harder and harder to keep. My feelings for Senquena, for example. If I tell her, there is no way to stop her from being hurt.*

"You don't seriously believe that," Eramine's eyes rounded. "How could it hurt anyone to know that someone cares about them?"

Look what happened to Lady Senmani, Rulraeno sighed.

"That's one person," Eramine put her hands to her hips. "There are plenty of others out there who have found happiness, I'm sure."

None like me, Rulraeno sobbed and folded her wings against her chest as she bowed her head. She saw no point in hiding the truth, so she confessed, *Cully, when he was alive, told me that his son was the*

97

result of a mistake he made as he tried to hide what he was from the world. He didn't act on his feelings afterwards, he said, because he hadn't met anyone he loved more than his son. So, while he lived, there was one other Onizard who was gay like me. But he is dead now, and I am alone.

"You can't be alone!" Eramine shook her head. "I refuse to believe you are the only gay Onizard out there. Surely there are others you just haven't met."

Joinmates are approved by one of the four Children of Light, and are announced and celebrated by the Sandleyr at large, Rulraeno sighed. *If there is anyone else, they are as quiet as I am about their feelings.*

"That makes no sense; you said the Fire Queen is gone."

She is gone, but her memory is there, and her allies are quietly hiding in the shadows.

"All the more reason for you to be proud of who you are. Look at a Quena!"

I do, Rulraeno said.

"No, really look at her!" Eramine crossed her arms. "She has made comments like she is unhappy and hates herself. She recites that Code of Earth of hers like it's her version of your swimming. Maybe if you told her the truth, she'd have greater hope and would have an ally. Maybe she thinks she's alone, too."

Rulraeno sighed. *Even if that were true, it wouldn't be fair to bring her into a spotlight she doesn't want, and to subject her to ridicule for something beyond her control.*

The stars were fading, and as she spoke, Rulraeno watched the light of Senbralni hit the field around them. At first, she thought there was a trick of the light, but then she realized the golden glow of the field was not from the light alone, but from flowers. Thousands of flowers, and all of them were the color of Senquena's eyes. Beautiful.

"You see," Eramine said as she stared at the vast field before them. "Even Senbralni and Maerno think it's time for you to tell the truth. Why else would they protect the flowers my family once grew, but not the sea grass?"

What if telling makes her hate me? Rulraeno whispered, though her eyes were lingering over the flowers.

"If it does, then she's not who you thought she was," Eramine shrugged. "Better to know that instead of pining for someone who doesn't deserve it. Besides, you have your family if you need help."

Sure I do, Rulraeno shrugged. *The aloof Leyrkan brother who is afraid to talk to me, the bitter lonely brother, the innocent sister, and the parents who speak in wisdoms alone. I am afraid Quena is my only friend.*

"No, she isn't," Eramine smiled and held out her hand. "You have me."

Rulraeno reached out her tail to Eramine's hand and held it in place as Eramine placed her hand on one side of Rulraeno's tail fin. The two held in place for a moment as Senbralni's light grew brighter.

Very well, Rulraeno said. *I am ready. I will tell her the truth.*

Chapter 18

"Senquena, you have to come see this place I found!" Eramine laughed as she ran toward the shore where the Child of Earth was standing. "It is so beautiful!"

I suspect you are plotting something, Senquena laughed. *Is Rulraeno at this beautiful place, per chance?*

"So what if she is?" Eramine pouted. "She deserves to see beautiful things as well."

Of course, Senquena smiled. *Very well, I will go see this place you have found. This is the most enthusiastic that I have seen you on this journey.*

"That's because I think you will like it," Eramine skipped toward Rulraeno, who was standing awkwardly with her wings tightly against her side.

Rulraeno, this place can't be as amazing as Eramine says it is, Senquena laughed as she stepped over the hill and stared at the ground around Rulraeno.

Flowers by the hundreds grew from the earth, and every one of them was golden in hue like

Senquena's eyes. Beautiful? Maybe, but it was hard to tell with eyes which were wet with unbidden tears as Senquena took in the scene before her.

I don't know, Rulraeno said softly. *I think it's beautiful because it brings out your eyes.*

Senquena felt as if there were boulders where her chest and head should be, for she couldn't breathe or think properly. Her heart was fluttering, her mind racing. She felt as though she were drowning in the flowers around her, even though in her mind she was admonishing herself for the obvious overreaction. Oh stars, oh stars, oh stars, they were all watching and judging her and she had to escape! But she couldn't move, she couldn't breathe, she couldn't feel anything but fear!

Stars, she gasped, shuddering and shaking as she kneeled down to try to make sense of what was happening. *Help...*

"We have to get her away from here!" Eramine's voice was somehow clearly audible in spite of everything that was happening. "Is she allergic to the flowers? I'm so sorry!"

No, Senquena moaned as her breaths came in gasps. *The flowers...don't hurt...but the claws...stars...*

"Claws?" Eramine sounded as confused as Senquena felt. "What claws? Is she having a panic attack?"

Quena, listen to me! Rulraeno said as she wrapped her tail around Senquena. Frissons of joy in a world of pain and fear. *I am here,* Rulraeno said calmly. *The claws are not. They can't hurt you. I...I will protect you. Always.*

I am...not...Senkanna! Senquena gasped and shuddered. *Rulrae, I am not...*

102

Of course you aren't Senkanna, Rulraeno said as she stared toward what seemed to be invisible enemies.

Then Senquena knew she had truly lost her mind, for she wasn't seeing flowers or Rulraeno anymore, but she was staring up at a pair of Onizards, one of which she recognized as Rulsaesan. The other Onizard, who was evergreen in hue, bore a striking resemblance to Ransenna, Cully's Bond who had been dead for years.

Please, forgive me, the evergreen Child of Earth pleaded, her head bowed and her wings tightly against her chest. *I deserve to be a non-nature for my crimes. Instead, I am Bonded into your family while the human girl who saved my life is dead. It is unfair.*

You are right, Rulsaesan said with disgust leaking into her tone. *It is unfair, and unjust. Even if I were to declare you a non-nature as you deserve, your non-nature status would not bring any humans back to life, so anything you do would never be enough to earn the forgiveness of those you harmed. Your mother would be ashamed of you, Ransenna.*

I know, Ransenna sobbed and shuddered as if she had been struck. Senquena shuddered as well, wondering why she was seeing a ghost and what they were talking about.

Furthermore, if rumors are true, you cannot be trusted around young Onizard men either, Rulsaesan said.

Rumors are false, Ransenna shrieked. *I-I don't even want a joinmate of my own anymore,* she added with a sigh.

I sense that isn't true, Rulsaesan said softly. *Nevertheless, I still choose to trust you in spite of your crimes. You are Bonded to my son. You will be his protector for as long as you live. That makes you my family.*

You don't want me as family, Ransenna sobbed. *I am a curse.*

That isn't true, Rulsaesan frowned. *You have spent too long speaking to the Fire Queen, no doubt. You will never be completely forgiven for your actions, but you can save a life today.*

Both Onizards turned toward Senquena, their expressions filled with concern. Except, they were not really looking at Senquena, were they?

Mama, what is wrong? a young child's voice shook as she tried to process what was happening.

Rulraeno, darling, you are going to have to be away from us for a while, Rulsaesan said softly.

Why? I don't want to go! I want to stay with you! Rulraeno squeaked.

I know, Ransenna said. *But there is a mean woman who will think you are a threat, and for that she will try to kill you if you stay.*

I won't be a threat! Rulraeno said cheerfully. *I won't be, and then I can stay. She won't kill me if I choose not to be a threat, right?*

You don't get to choose, Rulsaesan sighed. *None of us do. So you must hide, but I will be with you as often as I can be.*

But Mama, I won't be a threat! Rulraeno cried. *I can promise I won't be!*

Come with me, Rulraeno, Ransenna said as she scooped the hatchling up and placed her gently on her back. *Cully and I will make sure you are safe.*

But I won't be a threat! Rulraeno screamed. *I won't, Mama! I promise!*

Rulsaesan turned her head, and the memory was incoherent with screams and tears and promises that were impossible to keep.

104

But now Senquena was in a circle of strange Onizards on the floor of a massive cavern. The walls were littered with entrances to leyrs, some of which had Onizards looking out in confused interest. This was Invitation Hall, the center point of the Sandleyr and traditional gathering point for finding out who was Invited and destined to watch the next generation of eggs hatch. It was, based on the way the sun was directly on the floor beneath her, about midday, and a few more Onizards had gathered to see the commotion coming from her direction.

Her direction? No, this couldn't be right. Since when has she been Rulraeno's shade of deep blue? For that matter, when would she ever willingly be the center of attention?

My name is Rulraeno, daughter of Rulsaesan, and I challenge you, Fire Queen! Rulraeno shouted, yet the voice seemed to be coming from Senquena's head. Clearly she was in Rulraeno's memories, but why and how?

There's no Fire Queen here, you idiot, a random Child of Water shouted.

Then where is she? Rulraeno asked firmly, seemingly ignoring the insult. *I will defeat her and bring our Sandleyr peace!*

We already have peace, a Child of Earth said. *Your brother saved us all.*

What rock have you been living under? A Child of Fire cackled.

Everyone was laughing...every last one of them. Rulraeno was surrounded, and just like that, all the work she had done to hone her physical form to its full potential was for absolutely nothing. She had been hidden away for so long, and for what? She had all the Sandleyr staring at her, laughing, and she didn't have anything else to say. Her preparations were for nothing.

Senquena could see Rulraeno's tears and feel her own tears falling at the same time.

Oh my stars, Rulraeno! You're back!

Rulraeno looked up to see a Child of Wind running towards her before he pulled her into a strong embrace. *It's me, Delculble. Just play along, little sister,* he whispered.

I am back, Rulraeno said softly. *I am confused.*

Of course you are confused, the Child of Wind laughed loudly, for the benefit, it seemed, of the rest of the Sandleyr. He spoke loudly as well as he continued, *You have been in hiding for so long I think Mom and Dad forgot where you were. I am so glad to see you are back and ready to defend the Sandleyr against its enemies. Can you imagine, spending your childhood hidden from the world? We owe you a debt we can't repay.*

I wouldn't ask for repayment, Rulraeno bowed her head. *The Fire Queen is truly gone?*

Yes, the Child of Wind said. *By a miracle, she is gone. Everyone forgets how close to losing Senrae we were. We would do well to remember that less than a year ago, Rulraeno would have been locked in a fight to the death to try to save us all. I am proud of her bravery. You all should be too.*

Senquena didn't have enough time to process this scene before she was seeing another in front of her. She was in the woods, and she was seeing...oh stars, Delculble! His lifeless form was on the forest floor, and it didn't take a Child of Earth's knowledge to see he had been there for a few days. Carrion birds were trying to take advantage of the opportunity in front of them, and...

106

NO! Rulraeno half-screamed, half-sobbed as she charged the foul creatures, scattering them in all directions. Then, she turned back and nearly jumped. His eyes were watching her, even in death, and he looked frightened. He had been afraid, even though Delma said she comforted him. Afraid, and without his Bond, his son or his siblings. Stars.

Rulraeno cradled his head and the memory blurred to nothing but the sounds of Rulraeno sobbing over her lost brother. He had saved her, and she couldn't return the favor. Useless. Useless.

"Useless? Who told you that nonsense?"

Senquena blinked and found herself looking up to an umber-skinned human man with a warm smile and an open hand. It was Marinel, though Senquena had no idea how she knew this, or why it filled her heart with familial love.

"They said I'll never sail, and that I should give up!" Eramine shouted, before she grabbed his hand and stood. Senquena realized she was now somehow in Eramine's memory. "Maybe I should. I could be doing more productive things. I don't know how to shoot the bow as well as True, and I can't navigate the ship like Jamarius can. How am I supposed to lead when the time comes?"

"Don't stress over it. You have everything you need," Marinel said.

Confusion filled Eramine as she said, "What are you talking about?"

"This," Marinel said as he lightly tapped Eramine's head. "You have both smarts to figure things out and the imagination to use it properly. Also, you have this," he said before pointing to Eramine's heart. "Love and compassion are deep within you. You are honest as well. The only thing left to test is your

107

courage, but I am willing to bet all my cargo you have that as well."

"Then let me go with you this time," Eramine said. "I want to help."

"You can help by keeping True company." Marinel glanced around. "She thinks this is another supply run. We will gather food stores, but the real reason we are sailing is so that I can find a special surprise. It will be ruined if you go."

"A surprise?" Eramine grinned. "Okay, I will stay. But only if you help me gather these materials."

"It's a deal," Marinel said.

Then, as if by magic, he was gone, and Rulraeno and Eramine were back with her, in the present, shielding her from seeing her surroundings. Senquena's breathing was getting close to normal again, but her chest felt heavy and her mind was full of questions. Rulraeno and Eramine each looked as if they had seen a ghost.

What in all the stars just happened?

Chapter 19

What in all the stars just happened?

Eramine didn't have an answer for Senquena's question, only a fear of what she had just seen. If this was what life in this Sandleyr was truly like, then she was not traveling there to rescue her future Bond, but an entire people caught up in absolute foolishness.

"I saw...the past," Eramine said cautiously. "At least, I think it was the past. It was a confusing, emotional mess. You were having a panic attack, and then..."

When Rulraeno had reached out to calm Senquena down, both Onizards had gone into a trance. Neither of them looked like they were mentally in the present, and both of them looked as if they were having a nightmare of some kind. Both of them were shaking and in tears, and Rulraeno looked as if she were trying to get away from Senquena's side.

Eramine knew then that she had to break the two of them apart to stop whatever was happening to them. She couldn't let them suffer this way! Shoving a giant Onizard tail aside was not an easy task, and as she moved between them, she suddenly realized what the commotion was about.

***

Delculble was dead, his corpse picked apart by carrion birds and stars knew what else and Rulraeno would have to be the one to bury him because, stars, how could her family see this? How could she tell them this had happened to him? She should have been there to rescue him before this happened. Stars, why did this happen?

Eramine tried to reach out to comfort Rulraeno, mortified at the sight of the dead Onizard, but suddenly she was somewhere else entirely.

Senquena, you should wear these flowers to the dance tonight, Senquena's mother said as she held out a necklace of the flowers that Eramine had seen in the field previously. But, based on the towering structure in the distance and the shoreline around them, they were not in the field at all. Also, how did Eramine know who Senquena's mother was?

I don't know, Senquena bowed her head and folded her wings close to her side. *It seems a little much.*

Oh, but they bring out your eyes! Senquena's mother squealed. *And I want you to look pretty tonight, my only daughter!*

Daughter? Senquena's eyes filled with tears, and she sounded surprised at the word. If Eramine wasn't already completely confused, this would have been what brought her to that point.

110

Well, I did give you life, Senquena's mother laughed. *Come on. I heard that pretty girl you have a crush on is waiting for you.*

Something simply wasn't right. Eramine couldn't pinpoint it, but there was a feeling of unease even as the Senquena in the memory was happily putting on the flower necklace and following her mother. Senquena in the memory had a racing heart from nervousness, presumably over the crush. For the first time in this insanity, Eramine could almost sense the rapid breathing of Senquena in her present-day panic attack.

It didn't take long to know why; in the memory, someone jumped out at her and knocked her to the ground!

Oh my stars, what are you doing, Senkanna? the offending Onizard, a fellow Child of Earth, laughed as she stared at the flower necklace. *That stuff makes you look like a girl!*

Eramine blinked a few times as Senquena in the past and present trembled. *I am a girl, and I am not Senkanna.*

You could have fooled us, another Child of Earth laughed as he landed nearby. Senquena's father held out his tail as if he were offering to lift Senquena up, but promptly yanked it away again as she reached out with her own tail.

He actually believed me when I called him my daughter, Senquena's mother cackled, and Eramine wanted to punch her in the jaw. *Your Dad and I are*

111

tiring of this game, Senkanna. We are here to heal you of this delusion.

It isn't a delusion, and I am not Senkanna, Senquena said firmly, before one of them knocked her down again with their front leg. This time, there was a wound in her shoulder from claw marks.

Oops, Senquena's father laughed before he healed the wound. *We did promise we would make sure he didn't stay hurt.*

"No!" Eramine tried to scream, but there was no sound. Frozen in the past, she was forced to watch the monsters repeatedly slam their tails against Senquena, all the while laughing and calling her this strange name of Senkanna and insisting she was a boy. What was this madness?

What is this madness? A female Child of Water shouted as she ran to the scene in the memory, her words seemingly echoing Eramine's thoughts. Or perhaps Eramine's thoughts were echoing the memory, which meant she had to escape!

Dartenno, help me! Senquena screamed in desperation and pain.

Oh, it's Senkanna, the Child of Water frowned before turning to Senquena's mother. *You are sure this will make him realize his true self? It sounds and looks like torture. I knew you were going to try to talk sense into him, but this...*

It is the only chance we have, Senquena's mother said. *He is insistent on his delusion of femininity. Reason isn't working. We have to try to force this out of his system. We need to make him*

112

realize he is a boy so he can potentially be a proper joinmate to you.

You are sure this will help him? Dartenno asked. *I will stand guard for you if you are certain, but if there is a chance you are wrong...*

Senquena knew then that she had no friends in the world, and that now was the only chance to flee! Quickly, she healed her wounds as the two Onizards were arguing, and took flight, as far away as she could. Stars, her own family was against her, and so was Dartenno! No one loved her for herself, and no one would! Stars, what was the point?

Eramine was overwhelmed by the sadness of the memory, and knew she had to fight it with memories of her own. Quickly, she thought of one of the many times Marinel had taught her to believe in herself, and concentrated on that with all her heart.

Luckily, it was enough.

***

Eramine watched Senquena for signs of another panic attack, but the Child of Earth merely seemed resigned, though still upset.

I saw the past as well, Rulraeno said. *I have heard of this power to share memories, but only with Children of Light. If that was a real memory...*she trailed off as she saw Senquena's distress.

I saw the day you found Delculble's body, Senquena said, her mental voice shaking as she trembled. *What did you see?*

Your awful family, Rulraeno said. *You told me about it before, but seeing it...stars, I just want to hug*

113

you, but I don't want to do anything without your permission.

Senquena bowed her head as a single tear streamed down her cheek. *I would like that very much, but first let's get away from here. I h-hate flowers.*

Of course, Rulraeno said as she carefully guided Senquena out of the field of flowers. *Eramine, we owe you a great debt. It would seem that since you didn't have a traumatic memory like ours, you were able to help us escape. I saw your brother's love, and it snapped me out of it. But what did you see?*

"I saw both things you saw," Eramine said softly. "I wish I had been there in time with the cure, Rulraeno. I am going to plant a garden of it in Delculble's memory as soon as I get the chance. We can even plant it on his grave if you can stand going back there."

He would have liked that, Rulraeno sighed before glancing about anxiously. *How much of Quena's memory did you see?*

"Enough to know I hate Dartenno and your parents," Eramine said as she turned to Senquena. "What was wrong with them?"

Senquena sighed. *Technically, nothing. They were trying to help me.*

"They most certainly were not!" Eramine shouted. "They were conspiring to hurt you just to change you into someone else, someone who doesn't make any sense!"

114

Senquena glanced over to Rulraeno before she said, *They were trying to hurt me, yes, but only because they think I am mentally ill.*

"What on earth are you talking about?" Eramine snapped. "That makes even less sense!"

She's right, Rulraeno said. *None of what they have done is normal, and none of it makes sense. You obviously aren't mentally ill, only afraid of what they have done to you. Why do you defend them?*

I am not defending them, Senquena sobbed. *I just have to try to think there were some good intentions in them. It was just my mother's stupid idea to help me. I have to believe there was some room in her heart for love for me, because if my parents couldn't even love me, who else could?*

Rulraeno stilled, then bowed her head.

"No," Eramine said. "Anyone who hurts you on purpose is your enemy, not someone who loves you. Frankly, nothing of what I saw was even remotely good-intentioned. There was nothing but a lot of cruel idiots calling you a boy."

Senquena shuddered as her tears fell to the earth. *They were just going by their perspective. I hatched with a boy's body.*

Eramine blinked a few times as her mind processed what that meant. "But you're a girl."

Yes, Senquena said. *I am a girl, and always have been, but-*

"They didn't know what they were talking about, then," Eramine cut Senquena off, as any 'but' in this case didn't make any sense. "You are a girl. You know better than anyone else."

Not everyone believes the same as you do, Senquena said, before she folded her wings even tighter to her side and hid her tail underneath her legs. *When...when I was born, my parents...examined me...thoroughly...and then they got angry at me for lying about my gender. That was the first time they hit me.*

They...what? Rulraeno's claws dug so deeply into the ground, the earth around her started to sink.

I've grown too tall now, so they can't hit me anymore, but they won't call me anything but Senkanna.

"Why?" Eramine asked as she threw her hands up in the air out of exasperation.

The Child of Earth bowed her head for an uncomfortable moment. *It is complicated, and involves explaining our ancient language in a way that may bore you.*

"I want to learn your language!" Eramine said. "If what you say is true about my Bond, I must learn all that I can if I ever have a prayer of fulfilling my purpose."

There are words that have stronger meaning than first appearances, Senquena explained as she lifted her eyes but kept her head bowed. *Kan is the deepest, most selfless layer of the heart. The...male heart.*

Eramine took a moment to understand. "So 'que' is the female equivalent?"

116

Yes, Senquena said. *So when they call me Senkanna, they imply that at my core, I am a boy, and unchangeably so.*

"Then they are idiots!" Eramine shook her head.

I agree, Rulraeno said. *And anyone who would treat you with that kind of disrespect will have to answer to me.*

You are both kind, Senquena lightly touched Rulraeno's shoulder with her tail. *I am lucky I wasn't made a non-nature at birth, though. I still could be made one at any time.*

"Non-nature?" Eramine wasn't sure what the word meant, but she was certain that she wasn't going to like the definition any more than she liked Senquena's scumbag parents.

A non-nature is someone who goes against their natural state, offending the Great Lord of the Sky, Rulraeno frowned at the definition. *As punishment, they are forbidden to use their powers and must serve all other Onizards. This state must be declared by the ruler of one of the two kingdoms for it to be true. In other words, Quena is obviously repeating a lie someone told her, because there is no way that would ever happen.*

How is it a lie? Senquena braced her shoulders. *My parents told everyone I was delusional. They would only have to ask for me to be declared non-nature for going against my theoretical male state.*

When you were born, Leyrkan Mekanni ruled the Night Kingdom, and my mother ruled the Day,

117

Rulraeno said. *Mekanni's daughter-in-law spent a decade as a non-nature due to some awful trumped-up charge, so the idea of Mekanni using that as a punishment for anyone is a huge stretch. As for my mother, if she saw what I saw, those scumbags would be the non-natures, not you.*

"Besides, if you are a girl, saying you are a girl isn't going against your nature," Eramine said. "You are what my kin call Trueform."

Trueform? Senquena blinked.

"We take longer to talk than you guys apparently do, and we recognize that sometimes we make mistakes in identifying someone's gender based on what they look like when they are born," Eramine said. "So when someone tells the truth about who they are, we recognize their integrity and their heart and call them Trueform. That's how my brother's love got her name. She chose to be called Trueform because she's proud of who she is, and we are proud of her for being Trueform."

If only our people were that accepting, Senquena sighed.

"Acceptance? That is easy," Eramine said. "You just have to treat someone with respect. Being brave enough to tell the truth in spite of fear should be respected, not punished until you become depressed for being yourself."

I was depressed before that happened, but they beat me for so long that I wasn't fully rational anymore. Senquena said. *I had started to develop a crush on Dartenno before that night, but she obviously*

118

destroyed it. Can you believe she wanted to befriend me again?

I can, Rulraeno said. *She probably felt guilty and wanted to make amends. But what she did was unforgivable.*

Senquena nodded. *The worst part was that I wanted to die. And no, I am not talking about wanting to hide in a corner until people forgot about me. I flew to the highest point of the Sandleyr walls and was preparing to hurl myself on the jagged rocks that stick every which way out of the water below. It angers me that they made me consider it.*

"But you stopped yourself, obviously," Eramine said cautiously. What did one say to a friend who had just admitted she once wanted to die? She had been prepared to help Rulraeno earlier, but seeing the reality of Senquena's memory and knowing for certain that it wasn't even the worst memory she could have seen was so heartbreaking she felt speechless. "That was brave to stop yourself, and I am glad you did."

Brave? Maybe; I certainly didn't decide to live for noble reasons. I didn't even make the choice on my own at first. I was just about to make the leap when I felt someone grab my tail. Then I turned, and saw Rulsaesan holding onto me. She said, 'Young lady, why are you hurting so?' Senquena paused as a few tears ran down her cheeks. *I was so stunned, so delighted that she recognized me for who I am, that I told her the truth. All of it. And she responded by telling me I was valuable, and that she would shield me from whoever was tormenting me. That she would help me find*

119

friends. Friends! I could scarcely believe it. But she continued by telling of her own struggles with depression during the time when the Fire Queen ruled the Sandleyr, and even before that time, when no one but Rulraeno's father noticed something was wrong. And for the first time I realized that I am not alone. I have value, and I can help others.

"Of course!" Eramine exclaimed, "you have been a wonderful help to me so far, and I am certain to Rulraeno as well!"

I intend to do more, Senquena sighed. *I could have died that day, over a simple patch of flowers and the words of a false friend. I cannot let that feeling happen to anyone else. I want to learn how we go from sad to suicidal, and how to stop it from happening. It is still a struggle that I will never truly escape, though; things that remind me of what happened, like the flowers, still give me panic attacks, as you can clearly see.*

"But you got through it, with the help of your friends," Eramine paused in thought. "Promise me you'll talk to me before you go to that scary ledge again."

She can talk to me as well, Rulraeno said softly. *And if you fall, Quena, I will dive after you.*

I will never give you a reason to dive, Senquena said.

The two Onizards shared a look that was as if the whole of the world was in their thoughts, and the other Onizard was at the center of that world. It broke

120

Eramine's heart that this unexpected trip to the past had apparently sapped away Rulraeno's courage.

"We should get some rest," Eramine said. "If those idiots stole the flowers from this place, this island can't be far from the Sandleyr. They don't strike me as the intelligent, adventurous types."

Certainly not, Rulraeno laughed nervously.

Senquena sighed before curling up tightly. *Thank you both...for everything.*

Chapter 20

"Marinel, you have to get some rest."

The captain shook his head as he kept his grip on the wheel. "Jamarius, they just left the Island of Graves. I saw them."

"All the more reason for you to get some rest," Jamarius sighed. "We are all going to be dropping anchor whether you agree to it or not. If you act like chasing after the monsters is more important than paying respect to the dead, I don't know if I'm going to be able to stop a mutiny."

Marinel's expression softened. "Of course we're stopping to pay respect. I am sorry if I ever gave the impression that I wouldn't."

"This hasn't been easy on anyone," Jamarius put his hand on Marinel's shoulders. "Trust me, I'm angry that they just keep staying one step ahead of us. But we know they keep heading north, and we know that Eramine will keep leaving clues for us to follow her. Beyond this island, we have no clue what is waiting for us, so now is the time we need to take to prepare."

Marinel nodded. "I have no intention of leaving before we tidy up the island and pay respect to the dead."

"For all we know, we'll be joining them soon," True said as she climbed up to the deck. "We've finished making the arrows, love. I've gotten the ink and instruments ready to chart out whatever we find to the north. If we do survive, any map we can create will make us rich while keeping other traders safe."

"Your dad, if he is feeling up to it, could probably help chart the land where he is from," Marinel turned the wheel as they approached the island to keep away from the reef that had convinced his father no invaders would be able to come. The idea would have been a sound one if they had been dealing with human, as there was only one real safe way on and off the island by ship, and it lead to a large natural cavern that was responsible for keeping this ship afloat when the entire village had caught fire all those years ago. Unfortunately, there was no real defense for a fire-breathing monster.

"Was this cave always cut off from the water?" Hasana called out. "Because we need to stop, the sand is piled up where you said there was a safe haven."

Marinel shouted out orders, and the crew lowered the sails as well as the anchor.

Jamarius ran to the mast, and called out, "She's right, Captain! The sand is piled up where there used to be a straight passage through. It looks like the current changed over the years. It's a pity."

Marinel sighed and put his hand to his forehead. "No, perhaps it is for the best. I don't want outsiders trying to colonize this place, disrespecting our dead."

"I don't like the ship being out in the open like this," True said. "The monsters could have friends waiting for us."

"Maybe," Marinel said. "But that is the risk we took when we set out. We are just as likely to be attacked going into any cave large enough for one of those creatures to fit into. You said the arrows are all ready?"

True merely nodded.

"I want everyone to carry their bow with them!" Marinel shouted. "Don't fire if you think you see Eramine, and if you must fire, try to draw the creatures away from the grave circle first.. We will all pay our respects to those we lost by avoiding violence over their resting places."

Jamarius smiled grimly. "Those of you who don't have kin buried on the Isle of Graves, stand watch over the ship, and warn us if you see anything strange coming."

"I'll sound the horn once for a strange ship, twice for flying invaders and three times for stormy weather," Hasana called down. Her family of seafaring fishermen had joined the village after the attack, making herself and a select few others unaffected by the past tragedy.

"Thank you, Hasana," True called back.

"I have the best rowboat ready for us," Arvid stepped forward and held out his hand for his daughter.

True in turn held out her hand to Marinel, and the three stepped on board the rowboat, with Jamarius joining them after he'd given the pulley system a final safety check.

No one said a word as they rowed the remaining distance to shore, though Marinel felt a surge of pride that his wife was having to slow down her pace for everyone else. He was learning new strengths about her every day, it seemed.

As they all stepped onto the sand bar near the cave, Jamarius frowned and pointed at several sets of tracks. The small, surefooted tracks of Eramine were curiously weaving both away and to the cave, and larger monster tracks fell to either side of hers. Eramine's tracks continued on into the start of the flower field, and Marinel started following them as if in a trance.

No one had bothered to control the flowers that had once been the primary trading commodity of their people, and so they now grew wild, covering almost every spare inch of usable soil. When he was younger and getting used to the trade routes, potential customers had insisted he come back here to share the valuable blooms that couldn't grow elsewhere. Yet Marinel had always refused; it was cruel to steal flowers from his parents' graves, and he loudly proclaimed it to all who gave him grief over it. They were fishermen now, and the best in the lands thanks to the help of Hasana's family. Marinel would forever take poverty over desecrating the gravesite.

Which was why, when they approached the circle of stones, he nearly choked in grief.

"By the diety, what happened here?" Jamarius cried out as he ran to a large expanse of flowers that had been, for lack of a better description, *flattened*. It looked like there had been a great struggle, a horrific wrestling match in which the flowers had paid the ultimate price. Someone or something had tried to right the blooms afterwards, but it was a fruitless effort. A large patch near the circle of graves was completely destroyed.

125

Arvid and True ran to the circle and knelt down by Resa's grave. Marinel for his part stood paralysed for a moment before he ran to his parents' final resting place.

Marinel was used to seeing the ugly stones that were a poor representation for the people they memorialized. He'd deliberately sailed here once a year for his people to pay respects. Yet he was not prepared for the new, carefully carved name in each grave.

"Eramine," Marinel whispered as he traced his hand over his sister's handiwork. "You confirmed who you are, and I wasn't there for the milestone."

Marinel felt a hand on his shoulder, and reached up to cradle his wife's fingers in his.

"A milestone for a milestone," True said. "She missed our wedding, and we missed her declaring her true self in the stone. She is forever their Eramine now."

Marinel sobbed and kissed his wife's hand. "She risked everything to declare it. We don't even know if she's alive now; that struggle down there happened after she told the world who she is. What if they are punishing her for it even now?"

"There's no blood," Jamarius said grimly as he kneeled down before seven graves and bowed his head in prayer.

"He searched the field for us before he joined us," Arvid said. The old man wiped a tear from his eye. "There's sign of a struggle, but Eramine's tracks lead away from the struggle as well. Whatever happened here, she is still alive. It looks like she kept them from disturbing the graves. My wife's flowers are still there."

"Praise be," Marinel bowed his own head in prayer, though he'd stopped believing in a high diety the day his parents died. If there was a time to ask for help, this was definitely it.

It felt like too short of a time before three sounds of Hasana's horn filled the air, and the landing party walked back to the ship as somber as they left it.

"We should remain anchored here tonight," Marinel instructed as he gazed at the stormclouds that had seemingly appeared out of nowhere. "We all need to save our strength for Eramine, not waste it on fighting the weather. We'll start out again at dawn."

Jamarius and Arvid nodded as if Marinel had just given the correct equation to the most complicated of math problems.

True wrapped her arms around him. "Come to bed with me, please. You need your rest as well."

"I'll be with you shortly," Marinel said as the rain started pounding on the deck, sending everyone scrambling.

"You're not seriously going to stand out here in the pouring rain, are you?" True gave him a look as if he had lost his mind.

Maybe he had. "I'm just going to double check to make sure everything is in hand. Besides, the rain will give me an excuse to take off my shirt for you."

True laughed and walked to the ladder. "Don't dawdle, sailor man," she said as she slipped below deck.

Marinel let the rain soak his clothes and cover his skin, and the tears he felt he had to hide from his crew came out in full force. He fell to his knees, and screamed into the wind in a feeble attempt to get rid of his impotent rage and grief.

It's not as bad as it seems, the wind seemed to answer back, and the unearthly blue monster returned, planting himself on the deck.

127

"Diety, you again!" Marinel shouted. "Go away, we want no part of you!"

I lost my mother too, Lord Idenno said softly. *She doesn't have a grave with flowers. To be honest, I don't know where my brother and sister-in-law buried her, but if I did I'd make sure the rain covered her grave and grew flowers as beautiful as your mother's flowers.*

"Shut up," Marinel sobbed. "Your fellow monsters couldn't even respect her, or anyone else. The fields are destroyed."

But the stones are not, Idenno said. *I don't think everything happened as you think it did. Did you ever consider they might have been overwhelmed by grief when they learned what happened here?*

"Of course not," Marinel scoffed. "Your kind didn't respect them while they lived. Why should I believe they respect the dead?"

Why should you judge an entire species on the actions of one?

"Because the rest of you did nothing!" Marinel screamed. "You watched a dangerous monster head out to set fire to an entire village of people that never did anything but grow flowers. You could have fought her, but you let her go."

Not everyone did nothing, Idenno said. *Why do you think I am dead?*

"Probably because no one could stand you."

Idenno's form mimicked a deep breath. *There was an innocent village of humans, set on fire for the purposes of luring our heroes into the open for an attack. I ran to rescue them, and for my efforts I had my wings burnt and two of my four legs broken. Then, the monster carried me away, torturing me each night in ways I dare not speak of, until one day a young man appeared to save me.*

128

Marinel frowned and squinted. "What was he supposed to do against her?"

His mind was Bonded to a powerful Child of Wind, too fast to be burnt, who taunted her and fought her until she caught him in a dangerous spot where if he moved, two innocents would die. So the young man prepared for the inevitable, and so did I.

"You expect me to believe you took a blast of fire for a human?"

I don't expect you to believe anything at all, Idenno shrugged. *I just tell the truth, because I am afraid of what is coming.*

"Your kind should be," Marinel said. "We are prepared for war, and we will save my sister."

What if it is your sister who needs to help save you?

"I won't let her," Marinel shook his head. "It won't happen, anyway. I don't need rescuing, she does."

I think we can agree to disagree, based on the way you were acting earlier, Idenno tilted his head. *But in case you were wondering, I am indeed making one last plea to stop the violence.*

"I knew it," Marinel scoffed. "Save your ghostly breath, we aren't changing course."

I'm not saying you should change course, only that you should reconsider visiting your sister with arrows flying straight away. I don't want anyone making needless sacrifices.

"A sacrifice is coming," Marinel said. "We knew it setting sail. I'm not afraid."

Save the sacrifice for when it is meaningful, Idenno said. *Not for a fight that isn't warranted.*

"If you're so smart, what makes a sacrifice meaningful?"

There comes a time at least once in everyone's life when they are faced with a terrible choice, Idenno said. *I don't say this to make you fear its arrival, for nothing will ever prepare you for it. It will appear without warning, and suddenly you will see before you two paths. One of them will be so obviously correct it will hit you like a bolt of lightning, and you will run for that path no matter what that choice will bring. You will gladly take that path, even if it leads to your own death.*

"And why is that, oh great purveyor of wisdom?" Marinel's voice practically dripped with sarcasm.

The alternate path leads either to the greatest harm of the ones you love the most or to the harm of a vulnerable innocent. I am confident if you chose that path, it would lead to the breaking of your soul.

Marinel thought to the time he had first held his infant sister in his arms, and had prepared to shield her from the flames with his own body. "It has already happened."

The spirit in the rain frowned. *Then you understand why I am dead, then, and why I would die again if I had to do so.*

"I do," Marinel said. "But that doesn't mean we are equals, or that I should trust you."

With that, the captain stepped to the ladder and climbed down to his quarters, where True had already stolen the covers. Marinel kissed her shoulder before lowering himself into the space next to her. Uncovered and uneasy, he drifted into slumber.

Chapter 21

Eramine opened her eyes to a wall of fire. She knew she should panic, but there was no heat to the flames as she would have expected there to be, and she wasn't having any trouble breathing, either. She saw a much younger version of her brother running away with two women and frowned.

"You didn't check to make sure my brother wasn't having a nightmare before you brought me here?" Eramine started chasing after Marinel without waiting for a response, for she sensed that following her brother was the only way she was going to get out of the dream properly.

We're lucky I could find him at all, her future Bond trailed behind her, floating along as if underwater. *I've had to dodge this nightmare a few times before; there wasn't time to wait for a dream, because his ship has nearly caught up to us. Why did you stick around the place of flowers for so long?*

"I will tell you later," Eramine said as she dodged a falling ember. "We were wrong about Senquena and Rulraeno. I thought they were just being shy, but they are actually scared of each other being hurt by awful Onizards that are bent on harming them."

The future hatchling scowled. *My mother will hear about this, mark my words.*

"We have bigger problems first," Eramine said as she watched a giant orange Onizard with frightening red eyes walk over them, unseeing. "That must be the Fire Queen everyone has been telling me about. She's cruel and she doesn't belong in this world anymore."

I quite agree, her future Bond shuddered. *I can't believe I'm related to her. She's awful!*

"She's the reason why no one will be reasonable," Eramine said as she surveyed the wall of flames and smoke around them. "She haunts everyone's memories but ours."

Stars, the part of your brother's dream that is coming up is going to haunt my memories even though I was never there, the child said as she shielded her eyes.

Eramine wanted to shield her eyes as well, but she couldn't take her eyes off her mother. She knew the woman who was giving a resigned, brave glare at the monster had to be her mother, for she had Marinel's eyes and nose. The woman next to her had to be True's mother, for they shared the same look when they were afraid.

Just what I need, the Fire Queen said as she stared at a bundle in young Marinel's arms. *Name it Erstai and I will let it live as my personal aide. It will be above all humans when it helps me raise up the next Heir of Senbralni.*

132

"Era...mine," her mother gasped.

Oh, I would be cautious, the monster said. *It would be the aide of royalty instead of a pile of ash, which is more than a human deserves. Just give it to me.*

"Her name is Era...mine!" a clear voice rang out in the dream, before a wall of flame engulfed the two women.

"Mama!" Eramine wiped away tears as she turned away from the carnage. "I have never been prouder of my name. I never knew what it meant. Why didn't they tell me how special my name is?"

The demon meant to call you the ancient Onizaran word for human as your name for the rest of your life, Her Bond shuddered. *The literal meaning is Two Legs. Stars I hate that fire witch.*

"Two Legs?" Eramine whispered as her tears stung her face. It was surreal crying while hearing herself cry as an infant at the same time. "Two legs are all she saw in them? In my brother? In me?"

She was terrible, her future Bond glared at the Fire Queen. *What she saw in you doesn't matter, for she doesn't matter. Not anymore. You're going to help me drive her memory away forever, right?*

Stars, tell it to pull itself together! The Fire Queen snapped at Marinel.

"Fine!" Eramine shouted, suddenly utterly certain of what she had to do. "You want me to pull myself together? Well I have!" she shouted as she stomped out to the space between the Fire Queen and her brother. "I am going to be a zarder, and they will gladly tell my story long after I die. You are nothing but an ugly memory, and when they do tell your story, they use it only as an example of what not to be."

Eramine, what are you doing? Her future Bond squeaked. I *have some control of the dream, but I don't know if I can stop her! No one knows what happens if you die in a dream.*

"Eramine," Marinel seemed to age before her eyes.

Oh, I would be cautious, the Fire Queen said.

"I hold the power here, not you," Eramine laughed as she met the Fire Queen's glare with one of her own. "You are dead, and I am alive. You can't form new words, only the memory of ones you've already said. Only one person here remembers anything you've said at all, and I'm not afraid of the words he might remember."

You grow bold, the Fire Queen frowned.

"You grow weak," Eramine laughed. "What are you going to do, try to burn me like you did my parents?"

"Eramine, no!" Marinel screamed as his vision of her infant form vanished, and the Fire Queen sent another wave of flames in Eramine's direction.

"Nope," Eramine held out her hand and dissipated the flames effortlessly. "In my dreams, bullies have no place. In my dreams, I make the rules! So I'm going to keep imagining a world where no one has to be afraid of monsters like you, then I'm going to wake up and keep working until that world is a reality. As for my brother, you have no right to his mind!"

134

Fear showed on the Fire Queen's face for the first time. *The blood must be washed from me.*

"Damn right it must be!" Eramine glared at the Fire Queen as the evil Onizard stepped back. "But your forgiveness will never be in the woken world, and we will always remember you as a murderous monster without a place in our world. As for the dream world...well, in my dreams, you frankly don't exist."

Eramine waved the Fire Queen's image away as her future Bond cheered and did somersaults.

"Eramine," Marinel smiled through his tears. "You are so much like our mother."

Eramine smiled back as she waved away the rest of the flames and replaced them with the flowers from the Isle of Graves. "Dreams should only have room for love, Marinel. So it's time to send the past away. I love you, and I appreciate everything you and True did to protect me, but it is time to move past these scenes of violence and stop contributing to them."

Marinel sobbed. "Eramine, why didn't you trick the monsters into delaying for a while? I would have fought for you."

"That would have been a mistake," Eramine thought of a chair and sat down. "The creature that attacked us was a monster, but the rest of the Onizards I have met so far have not been monsters."

I'm definitely not, squeaked the child. *I'm a baby!*

"The monster that attacked us is dead, and the Onizards that live now are our friends," she trailed off for a moment as she looked around expectantly. "For

135

example, somewhere in this dream, Lady Amblomni is working to help let me talk to you."

How did you know? a soft, unfamiliar voice asked.

Mommy! The future hatchling squealed.

"When I was a baby, True and Marinel would never let me out of their sight." Eramine shrugged. "I thought about it just now and realized that it didn't make sense for you to leave my future Bond to go wandering around dreamland by herself. Plus, the Fire Queen actually looked scared at the end, instead of just disappearing like I planned to have her do. I didn't know how to think of her being scared, and they said you were the one who defeated her."

Ah, a giveaway, the voice materialized into a lavender-eyed Onizard with black skin and a glowing orb on the end of her tail.

Marinel screamed and reached around as if he were trying to find a non-existent bow, but Eramine simply bowed before conjuring another chair and gently pushing her brother down into it.

How long have you been with us? The future hatchling asked.

From the beginning I've been helping you, Amblomni said gently. *I would never stop you from whatever dreams you strive for, but I will also never leave you without support if you need it.*

"I guess Rulsaesan was wrong about you getting weakened by all this," Eramine laughed.

Indeed, Amblomni said. *I am as strong as I have ever been. I will admit that I was worried at first when my child became determined to Bond to a stranger from across the sea, but after what we all just witnessed, my concern was unfounded. I have no worries about this daughter of mine, only of her eerily quiet twin who hasn't stood up for herself yet. The only thing I hear from her is that she has a surprise when she hatches. I don't like surprises unless we're talking about the surprise that was my existence in the first place.*

"There's time," Eramine shrugged. "I wouldn't worry about it. These things have a way of working out."

So wait, the child frowned and hung her head low. *I didn't do the dream travel myself? I thought I was making you proud with my strength.*

You did travel into the dreams by yourself, Amblomni said. *I am so proud of you! I was merely following behind you to catch you if you stumbled, but you haven't needed me, so you haven't needed to see me.*

So I am strong, her daughter squeaked in joy before doing another somersault.

"How am I dreaming this?" Marinel asked. "Is it that weird monster in the rain's doing?"

Weird monster in the rain? Amblomni tilted her head. *You saw a weird monster in the rain?*

"Well, he is my brother," Eramine said. "He has ties to your bloodline through me."

Still, it is rather odd that he's singling out your kin instead of you, Amblomni blinked a few times before looking to Marinel. *How is Father Rain?*

137

"This creature called himself Lord Idenno, though I'd rather call him Lord Annoying. He won't shut up about giving up the fight."

Yep, he definitely saw Father Rain, Amblomni laughed. *Welcome to the family, Marinel.*

"Nope, I want no part in this," Marinel said, before he pinched himself and disappeared.

Eramine teared up. "He has deypin arrows, and I told them you guys were weak to them."

What? Amblomni frowned.

"I didn't know any better," Eramine said. "I wish I could take it all back. Rulraeno and Senquena are still afraid of loving each other, and I'm scared someone I care about is going to get hurt or killed."

Death happens, Amblomni said. *And it hurts more fiercely than you can ever know. But you fought the Fire Queen and won, Eramine! Things, as you say, have a way of working out. Also, I wouldn't worry too much about Senquena and Rulraeno. They've been having some rather interesting dreams of their own while you've been attempting to talk some sense into your brother. I meant to ask them about your progress, but...well, best to leave them alone for now.*

"That's good news," Eramine smiled for a moment before she pondered the remainder of the journey. "The sooner I get to the Sandleyr, the better. I want to have a firm discussion with you and Senraeni about some non-natures I've learned about recently, but not in front of my Bond."

Aww, why not? The hatchling asked.

"I've already taught you the word 'damn'," Eramine said. "I'm not going to teach you the other curse words that I want to say about those jerks."

Amblomni giggled. *I appreciate that you don't want to corrupt my daughter at such a young age. If they are truly worth being declared non-natures, I'm sure either Senraeni or I will listen. For now, I will just wish you a safe journey the rest of the way to the Sandleyr.*

Eramine wished she knew why she felt like traveling to the Sandleyr right now was like wishing for the coming doom.

Chapter 22

We must be close to the Sandleyr, Senquena said. *There are Onizards on that island over there!*

Really? Rulraeno shifted her head to get a closer look, which was a difficult task while flying with a human on her neck. *That's odd. I didn't think that island was very popular. There isn't anything on it but sea grass and a large cave that you can't even see from the sea grass around it.*

"That makes it easy to see that she's right," Eramine said. "Oh, is that a flame on that dark red Onizard's tail?"

Child of Fire, Senquena said. *Their own bodies boast of their powers.*

"That isn't good at all," Eramine turned her head to the sea behind them for just a moment before she got dizzy. "The ship's sails are on the horizon! They'll for sure mistake him or her for the Fire Queen!"

We've got other problems, Senquena said. *There is a storm brewing to the west. I can see the clouds drifting over there. We have a few hours, but...*

We have to warn them, and get them back to the Sandleyr, Rulraeno said as she started to descend. *Children of Fire have died in rainstorms, and that place is nothing but a tiny barrier island that often floods.*

"Seriously?" Eramine shuddered. "This poor guy has no luck today."

Maybe he does, Senquena said. *I think he found your cave, Rulraeno. I don't see him anymore.*

Definitely not my cave, Rulraeno said shortly. *But yes, he did.*

The Onizards drifted the rest of the way to the island and landed carefully. Senquena looked around, her expression one of surprise.

You're right, Rulraeno, you really can't see the cave from the grass, Senquena said. *How fascinating!*

You haven't even seen the inside yet! the voice of another Onizard filled their minds as a Child of Earth lifted her head seemingly out of the ground. Her eyes were light grey and seemed filled with merriment. *I am over here, little sister!*

Amsaena! Rulraeno laughed. *You only hatched a minute ahead of me, and I am not so little anymore.*

No, but I may still have you beat in size, Amsaena lifted her wings and flew out of what Eramine could see now was the cave. When Amsaena landed, she waddled over to the trio, for her stomach was rotund.

Eggs? Rulraeno gasped.

Amsaena nodded, her grin filling her face. *It was supposed to be a surprise until Lady Amblomni's eggs hatch. I don't want my babies being accused of trying to upstage the Heir of Senbralni hullabaloo. They deserve a quiet life if they choose it.*

Stars, Amsaena, do we have bad news, Senquena said. *There is a ship of angry humans following us.*

Oh, Amsaena laughed. *Maybe one of my children will Bond one of them and calm them down.*

141

"I don't know," Eramine sighed. "My brother is one of them, and he thinks I have been kidnapped." After a moment's pause, she added. "Well, technically I was convinced to come against my will at first, but your sister and Senquena are nice Onizards. I'm Eramine, and I am willingly traveling with them now."

My name is Amsaena, in case you hadn't guessed from my sister and her dear friend calling me by it. I must confess you have the most confusing backstory, Amsaena shook her head. *See, this is exactly why I live on the outskirts of the Sandleyr with my Emmefi. No crazy adventures, no worry about the family name, just peace and quiet.*

It can be nice off on your own, Rulraeno admitted. *But it can be lonely, too.*

Not if you have a hottie with you, Amsaena laughed and turned her head back toward the cave.

You called? A large, dark red Onizard lifted his head out of the cave. His dark green eyes were trained on Amsaena after he briefly nodded to Rulraeno's group.

I could hear you walking up here, and I couldn't resist teasing, Amsaena laughed, before turning to Eramine. *Oh, do you know what a Child of Fire is? Emmefi is the tall, dark and handsome version.*

"I know a little about what a Child of Fire is, but I will leave you to judge his looks," Eramine laughed, but noticed Emmefi seemed to swell with pride when Amsaena commented on his appearance.

Diplomatically said, Emmefi nodded in approval. *Amsaena is the only one who has said anything of the sort to me. I think she's biased. To be fair, if you tried to get me to describe how beautiful she is we would be here all day, so I am biased too.*

142

Goodness, she'll think we're shallow, Amsaena blushed. *Joinmated for over a decade and still commenting on appearances.*

"No, I would think that you are well-matched if you are still flirting with each other after all that time," Eramine said. "But have you seen anything else interesting?"

Oh yes, Amsaena said. *We haven't been here specifically, but we have been traveling to the outer islands around the Sandleyr to see what we can find. This one is my favorite; I think it is an ancient Onizard site!*

What makes you say that? Rulraeno perked up.

We'll show you! Emmefi said. *This cave is much larger than it looks, and the light from my tail will illuminate it nicely.*

Emmefi ducked back into the cave, and Eramine climbed down after him. The way was relatively shallow at the entrance, but the further she walked down, the further away the ceiling got from Emmefi's head, until at last they were in a room with hundreds of drawings scratched onto the wall. Emmefi lifted his tail into the air, and the flame on the end of it lit the cavern, highlighting pictures of dancing Children of Water. The further along the wall, the more elaborate they became. One nearest to Emmefi looked almost real, but also somehow familiar.

You see! Amsaena exclaimed. *No one has ever mentioned these in our histories. This place must have been home to an important ancient Onizard.*

Rulraeno chuckled loudly as she entered the cavern. *Hardly. Sis, you found the drawings I did when I was bored as a kid.*

Amsaena gasped. *You did every last one of these?*

143

Rulraeno nodded. *Well, I couldn't fly away and couldn't properly protect myself, so I had to occupy myself somehow. But I also couldn't let myself be seen, so I made up things to do. Drawing myself on the walls doubled as a protection against getting lost in the cave.*

Ugh, that isn't fair, Amsaena giggled. *Well, I am glad you said something. I would have made a fool out of myself trying to tell everyone else about it.*

We both would have, Emmefi laughed. *Seriously, if you are this good, I will need to get you to decorate my children's leyrs for them. We love the work you did.*

It is beautiful, Senquena said softly. *How did you stay so carefully hidden? This cavern is massive, and it is surprisingly well lit even without Emmefi's tail.*

Rulraeno stared at the ground. *Ransenna piled about a year's worth of food at the entrance and hid me behind it.*

Eramine frowned in realization. "You were in the dark, alone the entire time?"

No, Rulraeno said. *There was a second entrance hidden behind my self-portrait over there, and it brought light in here during most of the day. I sealed it permanently shut the day I gained my powers, though. It brought the water up here when it was storming.*

Senquena was pale as she said, *How far up?*

Not far enough to harm me, though it did scare me the first time, Rulraeno shrugged. *Before you ask, Dad, Mom, and Ransenna didn't know. I know Ransenna wouldn't have brought me here had she known. The hole was barely child-sized; I think she meant for me to escape that way if the Fire Queen found me.*

144

Oh stars, Sis, Amsaena bowed her head. *I had no idea.*

I didn't want anyone to have any idea, Rulraeno sighed. *It's embarrassing.*

No, it isn't, Senquena said firmly. *It is a sign of your strength that you lived through that, yet you are still kind and brave.*

Rulraeno blushed. *Kindness to others doesn't have anything to do with that, and it is easy to be brave when you don't have a choice.*

Father and Mother should have come up with some other plan to hide you, Amsaena scoffed. *This one was too full of risks with not enough reward. Even their stupid hiding spot for baby Senrae made more sense than this place.*

I don't know about that, Emmefi shrugged. *I mean, they hid Senrae in an abandoned leyr right above everyone. That hiding place was just as stupid as this one would have been.*

At least he had help, Amsaena shook her head. *Stars, I remember Father flying out to find you and freaking out when you weren't here.*

There was a major reward for finding you, Emmefi said. *That's what caused me to learn that I like exploring. Then, eventually, Amsaena found the one hiding spot only I'd managed to find before. Some would say I found the wrong sister, but it feels so right.*

Amsaena laughed and grasped Emmefi's tail with her own. *I'd say you found the right sister.*

Rulraeno glanced toward Senquena for a moment before blushing. *You two practically emit sappiness. They really had a reward for finding me? I wasn't that hard to find. Dad must not have looked into the water or the rest of the island. I didn't leave here for another six months after I gained my powers. I wanted to perfect swimming in the ocean before trying to make it back to the Sandleyr.*

You can swim? Amsaena's jaw dropped. *You are lying about how high that water came up, aren't you?*

Rulraeno turned her eyes back toward the entrance. *It doesn't matter, I am stronger for it.*

You are probably the strongest of our siblings, if not the Sandleyr, Amsaena said.

Strength is only worth so much, Rulraeno shrugged.

Is that why you always look uncomfortable in unfamiliar caves? Senquena said, the slightest hint of alarm in her tone.

Rulraeno nodded and bowed her head.

You should have told me, Senquena said. *Stars, I feel awful.*

That's why I shouldn't have told, Rulraeno said. *As you said, the caves were necessary for our protection.*

Surely a ship of angry humans isn't worth causing you that much discomfort, Emmefi frowned. *What damage could they possibly do?*

Rulraeno lifted her head. *They have deypin, and means by which to fire it at us.*

Sky Lord! Amsaena wrapped her tail protectively around her stomach. *How close are they?*

Close enough that we were going to suggest you come back with us, Senquena said. *There's a storm moving in as well, so that doesn't leave us with a lot of options.*

I don't know if I will be as fast as you three, Amsaena's voice trembled. *Stars, the children...*

...will be fine, Emmefi said firmly. *We don't all have to fly back at the same time. Suppose one or both of you stays just long enough for them to spot you with*

146

Eramine, but far enough away that they can't hit you with the deypin, or get a good look at things.

"They would ignore the island and follow me," Eramine smiled. "You and Amsaena can hide here until everything is sorted out!"

It's risky, but it could work, Rulraeno frowned. *What if the storm brings the water into the only entrance to this cave?*

I can't lose you, Amsaena leaned against Emmefi, who wrapped his tail around her.

They will see him for sure if he waits with us, Senquena said. *But if he goes first, and Rulraeno and I wait...*

We'll have a healer following behind him, Amsaena can stay hidden, and we'll be as safe as anyone can be, Rulraeno nodded. *Emmefi, we had all better step outside now. Any later and they'll see us coming out of the cave.*

See you back at the Sandleyr, love, Emmefi nuzzled Amsaena before releasing her from his grip.

Be careful, sweetheart! Amsaena smiled. *My babies need their tall, dark and handsome father!*

Our babies, Emmefi corrected playfully, before walking outside.

Eramine followed the three Onizards after waving goodbye to Amsaena, her steps swift but cautious. The plan they made was going to be the best way to protect everyone, and it could possibly even bring about a truce before they reached the Sandleyr. It was the most intelligent thing they could do with the limited resources they had, and if timed properly it ensured no one would get hurt.

Why, then, did dread fill her heart?

147

Chapter 23

"Monsters, in the sky on the starboard side!"

Marinel heard the call, but didn't betray his alarm by running to watch them fly away. His concern was the island ahead of them, and the oncoming storm in the distance. After days of dodging them and flying as swiftly as possible away from the ship, why did the monsters let them get close now?

"Captain, what are your orders?" Hasana called out from the crow's nest.

Marinel stared at the tiny barrier island he had seen the creatures leaving from. It seemed barren and lifeless apart from the sea grass growing around it. It barely seemed like something worth landing on, unless the monsters were so tired they had to have a moment's rest. Yet they seemed to be flying away with full strength, and he could have almost sworn he saw

148

Eramine waving at him. Why did it seem like he was being diverted away from this pathetic patch of sand?

"Captain?" Hasana's voice was hesitant.

"Do you see anything unusual on that shoreline?" Marinel asked.

The young woman squinted, before shrieking in surprise. "There's a cave, Captain! Do you think there's something important in it?"

"I don't know, but we should drop anchor!" Marinel shouted. "Jamarius, turn us toward that island. I want to see what those creatures left behind!"

"Sure thing, Captain!" Jamarius shouted back as he turned the wheel. "Should we wake up True so she can go with you?"

"No!" Marinel didn't know why, but he felt like involving his wife in this expedition would be a mistake. Perhaps it was that weird dream he'd had with his sister gaining power over the monsters, but nothing felt right at the moment, and involving others in what could be a dangerous exploration didn't seem wise.

"It doesn't seem right," Jamarius said as the crew worked together to lower the anchor. "True is your wife, and you shouldn't keep things from her."

"I'm not keeping anything from her," Marinel said as he packed arrows and swung his bow around his back. "I'm protecting her and the entire crew by going down there first. If I run into trouble, sail away and don't turn back."

"But Captain…"

"No buts," Marinel grabbed a hold of the nearest rope and tied it carefully to the side of the ship.

"A captain has to look after his crew first. If there is something dangerous down there, I want True to be safe."

"She's not going to give up on you that easily," Jamarius frowned. "If something happens to you, she's active captain, and she'll never let us sail away from you."

"That's why I want her to rest right now," Marinel said. "If I find something strange, I promise I'll make sure that you have the best knowledge to rescue what's left of me."

"Is that supposed to reassure me?" Jamarius shook his head.

"No," Marinel said as he climbed down to shore. "It's supposed to keep you alert while I'm down here. I will be back as soon as I can."

The cave seemed decently lit at the entrance, most likely since it was facing due west and the sun was setting. Marinel was prepared to drop down into the cave, but found instead that it was at an angle where walking was possible. The cave floor seemed as if it had been recently disturbed by multiple sets of footprints, including a smaller set that was easy enough to recognize.

"Eramine," Marinel whispered as he noted the tracks leading both in and out. Well, he wasn't going to rescue his sister from here, and yet there was more to the tracks than originally met the eye. There were four monster size sets of tracks that lead into the cave, but only three sets of tracks went back out again. Worse,

150

the set of tracks that didn't have an equal were the firmest into the ground.

Marinel quietly removed the bow from his back as he crept further into the cave.

The light was growing dimmer, but Marinel could still see the images of dancing Onizards on the wall, each one of them gaining a greater complexity. Ahead of him, he could hear a strange shuffling noise and what seemed almost like muffled breathing. Marinel paused and noted the decorative artwork continued further along the wall, until it abruptly stopped around a large, Onizard-shaped shadow.

"Hello," Marinel murmured, and the shadow got smaller even as the breathing turned both faster and more shallow.

Marinel reached for an arrow from his quiver, but something kept him from grabbing it. Why was this Onizard staying behind, where it was certain to be in the most danger? Why would the two they had been pursuing wait until they were almost within firing distance before leaving the island with Eramine? Clearly a diversion away from this Onizard, but why? Marinel would have thought that it was because the creature was a great warrior, but she was clearly cowering in fear?

Please, a female voice entered Marinel's head, the very definition of agony. The Onizard's tail was wrapped around her large stomach, and her wings were lowered around it as well. *If you mean to kill me, please wait...*

"Why should I do a thing like that?" Marinel scoffed. "Your kind is dangerous, and would kill us all if you had the chance!"

Never! she said. *I would rather the world live without anyone wanting to kill anyone. A comfortable home, a family filled with love...do you not want these things instead of the war that would surely come if you killed me?*

"Of course I do!" Marinel hissed. "But my parents are dead because of a monster like you, and now my sister is lost..."

No, not lost, the Onizard shook her head and crouched lower, shielding her stomach further. *You must be Marinel. Eramine loves you, and spoke only of wanting to keep you from getting hurt trying to fight a battle none of us want!*

"How dare you speak her name!" Marinel grabbed an arrow, but regretted it as the Onizard shrieked and started shuddering as if she had already been struck.

*Please...wait...*the Onizard lifted her eyes and stared at Marinel as if she was trying to accept an unacceptable decision. *I have heard of why you are angry, and I know why you want your revenge. I understand, and I am not afraid to die. I have lived longer than some could dream of living, and I have lived a good life. I have loved, and am loved in return. But my children...they have not taken their first breaths yet. They haven't had a chance to make mistakes and learn from them. They haven't even heard enough how much I love them, even before knowing them. They* *deserve to grow as old as they can, and if it means I must die, I would do it to protect them. I just ask that you wait...please don't kill me until my children's eggs are safely on the Leyr Ground waiting to hatch.*

"Children?" Marinel hesitated as he looked closer at her stomach. Then he looked into the Onizard's eyes, and saw the same fear he had seen fourteen years before in his mother's eyes as she ran away from the fires, forcing herself to keep going even through contractions. It was the most selfless of fears, and as such it was the most powerful. The creature could probably defend herself if necessary, and in reality should have crushed him like an insect by now. But she made no move to do anything other than protect her belly, just as his mother had. Unlike his mother, though, the Onizard had the choice to fight back and kill him first, yet she only pleaded for her childrens' sake.

Marinel realized then that he was the monster he was fighting to destroy.

"Your people truly don't mean to hurt us," Marinel said softly as he placed the arrow back where it was drawn from and lowered his bow to the ground. It took all of his effort not to kick it across the cave floor.

No, The Onizard said. *Ever since the three zarders defeated the Fire Queen on three separate occasions, it is considered an honor among our people to be Bonded to a human. Your sister will be royalty in both of our kingdoms, and your people will be*

153

welcomed as honored equals if you visit the Sandleyr in peace.

"Marinel?" True called out from the entrance. "Did you find anything?"

Marinel winced, making a mental note to reprimand Jamarius later. "No, just random writing on the walls. Not from Eramine, though. This place is a dead end, and dangerous. I dropped my bow in a chasm." Marinel shared a pointed look with the terrified Onizard, then turned away.

"Come back to me then, dear," True called. "The wind is getting stronger. We have to choose; do we sail, or do we anchor here until the storm passes?"

"We sail," Marinel answered without hesitation. If blood were to be shed, he would not let his crew be the ones to do so.

Chapter 24

Eramine couldn't shake her fear that something was terribly wrong. She wanted to believe that the plan was working, and that everyone would eventually see reason, but she couldn't help but notice the sharp rocks surrounding the towering wall in front of her. Some of them were almost the size of her brother's ship, and there was no place to land except for a beach on the far outskirts of the wall. The storm was bringing fog, and she could not see anything to her left as a result.

"We need some sort of warning beacon," Eramine said as Rulraeno flew toward the top of the wall. "My brother won't be able to see the danger if the fog comes closer."

The ship is taking longer than we thought, Senquena said. *You don't suppose...*

"They are probably taking extra time to avoid any hidden reefs or shoals," Eramine said. "Plus, Amsaena would warn us if there was danger."

Of course, Rulraeno said as she landed on the top of the wall and immediately started staring in the direction they had come from. *I can see the sails, for now at least. They are coming, and the wind bringing the fog is bringing them here faster. We need a Child of Light, but sunset is the time between kingdoms, when my mother falls asleep and my brother wakes up.*

"Yes, but there is still fire," a human woman's voice called out from further down the wall.

Eramine turned to see a pale woman with bright red hair and brown eyes walking towards them carrying a lantern. Behind her, a brown-haired man with blue eyes and a thick beard followed closely behind, along with a grey Onizard with a fan of feathers on his tail. The Onizard's green eyes surveyed Eramine with some interest.

I see we have a welcoming party, Rulraeno said dryly.

"You know I wanted to be the first to meet her. We came as soon as Emmefi told us the news you'd be coming," the red haired woman laughed and stuck out her hand to Eramine. "My name is Jena."

"Eramine," she said her name simply as she took Jena's hand and shook it. Now that the woman was close, there was something weirdly familiar about her. Her face, if it was darker and slightly rounder, would have closely resembled someone else she knew. Wait, what was the story True's father told about joining her people?

"Are you okay?" Jena asked, one eyebrow raised as she toyed with a silver chain around her neck. "You look confused. Trust me, it may seem overwhelming at first, but the Sandleyr is a welcoming place, and you are a part of my family now. The man

156

behind me is my husband Bryn. He is a Zarder like me, and the Onizard behind him is his Bond Xoltorble."

Xolt, please, the grey Onizard shrugged. *We only stand on ceremony when it is demanded of us.*

"Which is more often than not," Bryn laughed. "Trust me, if you are nervous about all of this, I can assure you that Xolt and I have embarrassed ourselves so often that anyone else looks wonderful by comparison."

"Don't listen to him," Jena rolled her eyes, but there was a warmth about her as she gazed at her husband. "He'd talk of his clumsiness but gloss over the times he's saved someone's life or stood up to the Fire Queen herself without a scratch."

"I would not recommend doing something similar," Bryn said. "I only did that when I thought Jena was dead, and my mind wasn't in the right place."

Eramine smiled and nodded, noting that this was a story she needed to hear in more detail later. "It is lovely to meet you all, but my brother is sailing a ship toward us right now because he thinks I am in danger."

"Sounds like a good young man, if misguided. I am sure we will be friends later," Bryn frowned. "The fog...how will we see him?"

I have been tracking the ship while you were talking, Rulraeno said. *We can try to guide the ship away from the rocks, but we can't get too close.*

They have deypin, Senquena hung her head low.

157

Jena gasped and fell to her knees as Bryn quickly wrapped his arms around her. "No...we can't have more of that here," she sobbed. "If Senrae finds out-"

"I have the cure, and so do they if we can just talk them into peace," Eramine said.

The cure? Xolt stared at Eramine as if he had been struck. *Stars, you should have been here when my grandparents were ill...*

"It wouldn't have saved them," Jena sighed. "But it could have saved-"

I know, Rulraeno's gaze was indiscernible, though she seemed to freeze up as Senquena hugged her with her tail.

How sure are we that we can talk them into peace? Xolt asked. *We don't have much time; Cousin Amby asked me to be awake tonight in case the babies hatch.*

Xolt, you aren't safe on this wall, Rulraeno said simply. *You should take the zarders back to the Sandleyr before our guests arrive.*

"I want to meet our guests," Jena smiled as if she had been planning on inviting the ship's inhabitants all along. "Surely you don't think they could hurt us with the deypin without climbing up the wall."

Eramine's people can send deypin flying through the air on dagger-sticks they call arrows, Senquena sighed. *So yes, they could accidentally harm you while trying to hurt us.*

158

"Your people sound dangerously brilliant," Bryn frowned. "As much as I would like to meet them, Jena, your safety is more important to me right now."

Don't let him fool you, Jena. Your safety is always his second highest priority, Xolt laughed.

"Second highest?" Eramine scratched her head. "I thought they said they were married? What could possibly be a higher priority?"

"We have an eight year old son named Keegan," Jena laughed. "You'll meet him later; he usually waits to wake up until nightfall. He's loved the Night Kingdom since he was a baby crawling under Grandma Senni's feet. I'd have woken him up early to meet you, but…"

Rulraeno is probably right, Xolt shrugged. *The less people on this wall when they arrive, the better.*

"Maybe," Jena said. "But if I keep Eramine here company, surely they will realize humans are safe here."

"Or they could fire first and ask questions later," Bryn said. "I am not a gambling man."

Nor can I let someone else get hurt on my watch, Xolt sighed and folded his wings against his side.

"I'm sure whatever happened wasn't your fault," Eramine said gently.

I was young and reckless once, Xolt said. *I thought I could save everyone, but instead I wound up in the blast path of the Fire Queen. The only reason I am still alive is Lord Idenno jumped into the flames to shield me. Respectfully, it was my fault.*

159

"No," Eramine said. "Everything I have heard and seen tells me you would never have been able to rescue Lord Idenno. The Fire Queen killed my parents just so she could enslave me to protect the future Heir of Senbralni."

That was planned? Xolt frowned. *Everyone thought Amby was an accident, even those who knew the truth about her parents.*

"So you're an orphan, too," Jena frowned and gave Eramine a hug. "I am sorry. I'm sure your parents were brave."

"They were," Eramine said quietly. That nagging familiarity was just not going away. "Jena, how did you get to this place?"

Jena ran her fingers over her silver necklace. "The Fire Queen attacked my village. There was so much confusion and smoke, I know I must have missed death by inches several times, and that was only because my mom guided me out. But we were too late to escape; the demon cut us off from the water and herded us to the edge of a cliff."

"I suppose we were the lucky ones; she didn't kill us right away. She commanded us to climb onto her tail, and held it in front of us. Bryn pulled my mom and me up and we scrambled up the Fire Queen's back. There were some others who made it, but those who hesitated..." Jena buried her face in her hands.

"We lost almost everyone," Bryn said. "Xolt and I went back and found graves, so we know someone lived. But we never learned who, and we never saw the rest of our families again. As far as we

160

know, Jena and I are the only ones left to remember the place."

"Maybe not," Eramine said. "Do either of you remember a man named Arvid?"

Jena turned pale. "I remember him well. He was my father. We lost him in the attack."

Eramine's jaw dropped. "I don't know how to tell you this, but I think you are my sister-in-law."

Bryn guffawed. "Well then, all the more reason to keep this family reunion peaceful. What is the plan?"

I should get Randenno, Xolt said. *His dad has him standing at the Watchzard rock, acting as an apprentice. He'd love to have a chance to do something more useful.*

The two of you should only come up here if we give the signal that it is safe, Rulraeno said.

"Who is Randenno?" Eramine asked.

"He is Deldenno and Ransenna's only biological child," Jena said. "He was a bit of a surprise, really; we didn't know she was carrying his egg until she died. He nearly never hatched."

His father is overprotective, Senquena shrugged. *You can see Randenno down below; he's the little blue Onizard with the shorter than average legs standing next to the tall one who looks like Rulraeno.*

Eramine stared down the other side of the wall and noted in the distance two Onizards, one tall and the other short. The short one seemed anxious to leave but reluctant to do so at the same time.

161

Poor kid is probably hearing another story about his saintly mother, Xolt rolled his eyes.

His mother was a saint, Rulraeno frowned.

Yeah, but if he tries to be her instead of himself, he'll never be who he was born to be, Xolt said. *I am going to make up some excuse about Senraeni requesting his assistance.*

No, Senquena said, *tell his father that he is needed to help us welcome the new zarder. It's the truth, and an excuse he won't argue with.*

You are right, that makes more sense, Xolt said. *Senraeni doesn't need help most of the time, and Randenno is the adoptive uncle of the children, after all.*

Eramine frowned. "I am never going to keep the family tree straight."

"No one expects you to, dear," Jena laughed.

"No, they just expect me to save the Sandleyr by existing," Eramine shook her head. "I still don't understand everything, but I will do my best to help."

"That's all anyone can ask for," Bryn said. "Now, where is this brother of yours?"

Chapter 25

"Marinel, we need to talk."

Marinel looked up from concentrating on the wheel to find the entire crew had surrounded him. "What are you doing? These waters are bound to be treacherous ahead of us, and we're going to need all the teamwork we can to confront the monsters the right way."

"We don't think you are going to confront the monsters the right way, Captain," Jamarius said, his shoulders slumped in resignation. "You've been acting strange lately, talking to things that aren't there, not sharing things with True, taking needless risks on your own…it's just not like you."

"I haven't been talking to things that aren't there!" Marinel protested. "What on the furthest seas are you talking about?"

"I heard you," Hasana pouted. "I was in the crow's nest during that last storm, and you were babbling nonsense about not giving up the fight."

"It wasn't like that…" Marinel said weakly. "I was practicing a speech."

"That's just it," True said. "You've always been a man of action, not speeches. I love you for that, and I also love how much you care about your family."

"Then trust me," Marinel said. "I have a plan to confront the creatures. Let me speak as an emissary, while the rest of you wait in hiding with the freezeneedle arrows. If the monsters move to attack me, fire. But if they peacefully give Eramine back…"

"Captain, that is never going to happen," Jamarius scowled and held out his hand, his fingers outstretched. "Five. That's how many older brothers I lost to the monsters. I am the only one alive to carry on my family's name, and I risked all that to follow you."

"I will be grateful for that until my dying day," Marinel said.

"Not grateful enough," Jamarius snapped. "Look, Captain, we would follow you anywhere in your right mind, but we think your grief is overtaking your sense right now."

"True," Marinel pleaded as his crew stepped in closer. "True, do you trust me?"

His wife held him in an embrace that seemed to last an eternity. "Marinel, I love you."

"True, I-" Marinel began, before he attempted to reach out to caress her and found that his hands were bound. "True! What have you done?"

164

"I promised you integrity, loyalty, and heart," True said. "I'd be lying if I thought you were in your right mind right now, Marinel, and my heart is loyal to you. We're keeping you bound for your own good, so that you don't hurt yourself when we face the monsters."

"I can stop them!" Marinel shouted as his traitor crew bound his feet and placed him to the side. "I can stop them! Eramine is safe! She was in my dream last night and she told me so."

"Marinel, we can't rely on dreams to survive," True said softly.

"No, but sometimes they can guide us to do what is right!" Marinel shouted.

"Maybe," True said. "But sometimes they give false hope. I had a dream last night that we had a child together, a daughter we raised to do what is right. Her hair was as white as the clouds, and her skin was blue like the sky on a stormless day. Dreams aren't real, Marinel."

No, Marinel thought to himself, but the fear in that pregnant Onizard's eyes was real, and it was clear no harm was meant to come to their crew unless they struck first. But explaining that he let the creature go was likely to get him thrown below deck, and he needed to find a way to escape and take over the wheel again.

The clouds above them opened up, and rain began falling in droves. Gone was the protective shield they had been experiencing the whole voyage; instead, if it were possible, it seemed the rain was falling even harder on the ship.

The crew scrambled into position, some of them slipping on the wet wood. True kept her hands on the wheel, shouting orders for Jamarius to control the sails.

My, how did you get into this pickle? Lord Idenno perched on the rail beside Marinel, which would have looked comical if the situation wasn't so dire.

"This is all your fault!" Marinel shouted. "Show yourself to them so they know I'm not crazy!"

Sorry, kid, I can only appear to those with ties to my bloodline, Lord Idenno shrugged. *It's a stupid ghost rule, but I have to follow it. Anyway, we've got bigger concerns. Your wife is terrible at steering this thing and is a bad judge of character.*

True frowned and issued another order to Jamarius and Hasana.

She's steering you guys directly toward the rocks that killed my daughter's mother's father.

"Why don't you just say father-in-law like a normal person?" Marinel would have thrown his hands up in the air if they weren't bound together.

Because I prefer not to mention the non-relationship I had with my daughter's mother, Lord Idenno's face was grim. *I'd rather emphasize you are sailing toward rocks that are big enough to dash this vessel into shreds.*

True frowned again. "This fog is getting thick. Jamarius, slow us down!"

I'd also like to note how curious it is that you've been carrying on a conversation with me that your wife is pointedly ignoring, even though it would make you sound crazy to the average person, Lord Idenno said as he stared curiously at True before waving his tail in front of her.

True blinked each time the tail passed in front of her face, and her grip tightened on the wheel.

Hmmm...interesting indeed, Lord Idenno said. *Well, perhaps one of those cute babies from Lady Amsaena or...well, I'll wait before I speak the other possibilities. Don't want to jinx anything, and if what I'm thinking is correct, it will be a delightful bit of irony.*

"I don't know what weird sorcery is going on, but we are not going to leave this place without Eramine!" True snapped. "I'm not afraid of you."

No, I would not expect anyone to fear me. I'm dead, and I can't do anything, Lord Idenno shrugged. *But again, you have to turn away, or you are going to hit the rocks.*

"I don't take orders from monsters," True said firmly.

"Please, True, listen to him," Marinel pleaded. "I'm sorry I never told you what was really going on, but this creature is the reason why I knew how to navigate the shoals we were caught in a few days ago. He is also apparently able to control the rain to a certain extent. He could be our ally if we let him be."

"No, it is not my intention to give in to this...this thing!" True snapped.

167

For stars sake, put aside your pride for a second and listen to me! Lord Idenno was staring at the head of the ship now, and his tone had changed from jovial to frantic. *If you continue on this path, you are going to crash, and someone might die!*

"Better to die free than live as a slave," True's grip was even tighter on the wheel, if possible.

No, it is far better to live poorly than to not live at all, Lord Idenno said. *At least living poorly you have a chance to change things. But you really aren't going to have a chance at all if you continue on the path you are on right now.*

Marinel fought his bonds, but his crew was just too talented. If Lord Idenno was correct, and the rocks were directly ahead, an impact would send True flying directly into the wheel with no protection. The smooth wooden handles suddenly looked ominous.

"You are just trying to protect your kin," True said. "It's admirable, but we're sailing to rescue Eramine, and no one is going to stop us."

For stars sake, Eramine has already rescued herself! Lord Idenno snapped. *Please, just turn slightly to the right. There might still be a chance for you to catch a current and sail to the safety of the cove.*

"There is no safe place for us," True said. "We knew that sailing here. We all prepared ourselves to make our last stand, for Eramine's sake."

There's no reason for it! Zarder Jena is waiting on the other side of the wall to welcome you all with warm beds and a well-cooked meal.

"How dare you mention her name," True snapped. "Jena is dead. My father saw her die, along with his first wife."

Oh, Lord Idenno tilted his head as if to get a better look at True. *A connection to Jena might explain the connection to my bloodline. My brother did mix his blood with her Bond's blood to adopt him. Yet I thought...no, I know there has to be more to it than that. Look, Jena is alive, and she really is waiting for you guys.*

True wiped away a tear. "So this is the sorcery, then. It tells you what you want to hear to turn you away from the correct path. It told you that Eramine was fine, and it told me that my older sister is alive."

Oh, for star's sake...

"What if it isn't sorcery?" Marinel asked as he crawled toward the wheel. "What if he's telling the truth?"

"If it isn't sorcery, why is it getting stronger as we get closer to what it's supposed to be protecting?"

I live...I mean, I ghost in the rain. And you're fifteen seconds away from hitting the rocks head on.

"I don't trust it," True said.

"Then, trust me," Marinel said as he positioned himself between True and the wheel and closed his eyes. "True, I'll always love you more than anything."

The fog disappated just enough for a giant, jagged rock to appear in front of the ship. There was no time to turn the ship out of the way, and when impact made True slip on the wet deck, it was Marinel that she landed on.

169

Marinel's head, however, landed directly on the ship's wheel, and Marinel fell over in a pool of his own blood.

Chapter 26

It was unclear if True or Eramine screamed for Marinel first, or who screamed the loudest. What was clear was the lack of time that the man had if someone didn't intervene.

I am a Child of Earth, and this is my Code, Senquena's voice shook as stared at the sinking ship and the injured man at its helm.

No! Rulraeno reached as if to grab her tail, but Quena had learned how to dodge other Onizards, and now was not the time to be focusing on anything other than saving the humans. Judging from the blood visible from the top of the Sandleyr wall, there wasn't time to waste trying to convince Eramine's people of her intent to help.

She would simply have to show them, and save Marinel's life.

Senquena broke her recitation of the Code for the first time and only time in her life as she looked at

Rulraeno. *I love you, and I am sorry that I am breaking my promise to you.*

Rulraeno stared as if she had been told the location of a lost treasure. *Quena, I-*

Senquena took a deep breath and dived toward the sinking ship and the rocks, unfurling her wings to catch any drafts that would carry her safely to the part of the ship where Marinel was losing blood quickly. *I will heal without question or prejudices, giving preferences to those who have the worst wounds.*

The first arrows struck her side, trifles if she did not know about the deypin. It stung, but not nearly as badly as knowing she had to ignore Rulraeno's screams, even if they sounded suspiciously like *Quena, no! I love you too! Come back to me!* There was no time to concentrate on her own pain; there was only the Code. *I will not put myself above others, for my life is the Sandleyr's, and the Sandleyr is-*

Quena lost all thought of speech as an arrow hit her deeply in the neck. If her thoughts weren't on the pain and the task at hand, Quena might have admired the ability behind the shot, for the woman who fired it was doing so while her arms were still around Marinel. True seemed to believe Marinel was beyond saving, for she had a look of utter despair and anger in her eyes. Quena forced her concentration into healing the gash on Marinel's head, even as she felt a sharp pain in her tail. So this was what a knife felt like; well, as much as it hurt, who could blame the poor human for defending her mate?

Luckily, even the worst human injury was much easier than healing an Onizard, and Quena had practice healing under harsh conditions. Marinel sat up and opened his eyes, only for True to jump back and scream as if she'd seen a ghost.

My life, Quena whispered as she lost strength in her wings and fell into the water.

Quena tried to copy the movements she'd seen Rulraeno making when she was swimming, but her legs ached terribly, and she could barely breathe. Strange that she had once wished for this end, for this was worse than anything her enemies had ever done to her. She was sinking, losing her control, and there was nothing but darkness below her. She could feel the fight leaving her legs, but she had to do something to try to stop the seemingly inevitable, so she did her best to swim.

She was failing terribly, and sinking quickly. So many rocks below, and dark depths where no one would ever find her bones even if they were searching.

A sudden splash beside her frightened her even more, until she saw a familiar blue form diving underneath her and felt Rulraeno lifting her out of the water and swimming for the two of them. Her strong and beautiful Rulraeno; it seemed silly now that Quena had ever thought hiding her feelings was a good idea.

I'm sorry, she said weakly. *Made you...dive.*

I would do it again, Rulraeno said. *I would always dive for you, my love.*

Quena tried to respond, but the pain was too great, and she could feel herself losing conciousness even as Rulraeno brought them to shore. If this was the last time she awakened, at least she had her dear Rulraeno with her.

But she didn't want to die, and she didn't hate herself, either.

Chapter 27

Eramine let go of the breath she didn't realize she was holding when she saw Rulraeno and Senquena emerge from the waves below. Instinctively she grabbed the pouch with the salveweed to assure herself she still had it. Good, now all she needed was to get one of the Onizards to carry her down and she could save Senquena's life.

Yet none of the Onizards were left on the wall; the fight had gone out of her people when they saw Marinel's miraculous turn from death's door, and the remaining Onizards were now concentrating on carrying them all to shore. By some miracle, no one else was seriously hurt; most had braced themselves when they saw the rock, and the crow's nest somehow remained above the chaos with Hasana safely tied in place. True and Marinel were the only ones left on the wreckage. But it was getting hard to see them as what light that had been breaking through the fog had disappeared, presumably as the sun was setting.

"Are you okay?" Eramine called down to her family, noting how odd it was they hadn't moved from where Marinel originally fell. Some of his blood had even stained their clothing! There was no need for the tired captain going down with the ship cliché; everyone was rescued, and everything was going to be fine as soon as she got to Senquena.

"I'm fine," Marinel shouted back. "I am not sure how, but I am."

"Next time, listen to me when I try to talk to you in our dreams!" Eramine snapped. "My future Bond has powers to help me talk to you and help you if we can't see each other!"

"That sounds great, but there's only room for one woman in my dreams, and she's on this wreck with me!" Marinel called back, before he embraced his wife.

***

True couldn't hold back her tears, and she didn't care who saw her. She also couldn't let go of her husband, even though she knew they would have to leave the ship eventually. It was a testament to their parents' craftsmanship that it was remaining upright on the rocks in spite of the giant gash in the side of it. But it was slowly sinking, and soon it would be no more.

Everything about their old life was gone now, and nothing made sense anymore. But it was an easy trade to make; even if the monsters did intend to enslave them, Marinel was alive.

"True," Marinel kissed her gently and wiped away some of the tears on her face after she freed him from his bonds. "It will be okay. We can rebuild and start a new life."

"I almost lost you," she whispered. "I felt your life slipping away from me, and it was all my fault. What's worse, I tried to kill the very creature who saved your life. I must beg for forgiveness, assuming she lives. I…I never miss."

"I think she granted forgiveness when she healed me," Marinel said as he took off his bloodstained shirt and threw it aside. "But I must beg you for forgiveness, True. I didn't trust you with what I had learned about the Onizards, and because of that we nearly died."

"I didn't trust you either, and you nearly died saving me," True sighed and leaned against her husband's shoulder. "I will never again make that mistake."

"I will never give you a reason in the first place," Marinel said, before the boards creaked around them. "Well, you always did hate how often I had to sail on voyages. Consider this a retirement, a late wedding present."

A strange present indeed.

True jumped back at the sight of a monster who was larger than the rest, and whose blue eyes stood out against his black skin. He held out his tail and the entirety of the ship was lit up with the orb on the end of it. His bearing was regal, but his demeanor emanated kindness.

My name is Leyrkan Senraeni, Bond of Zarder Jena, he said as he precariously perched on the edge of the ship. *I heard you needed rescue. Quick, climb onto my tail. This place is treacherous, and I fear sending anyone else down here.*

"Did you say Jena?" Marinel asked as he pulled True onto the Leyrkan's tail.

Yes, I have heard her name may be important to you, and I will take you to her in just a moment. This certainly one of the more confusing situations I've awoken to find myself in, Senraeni blinked a few times before looking over the fragile remains of the ship. *Is everyone else safe?*

"Yes," True stammered. "I gave the order to abandon ship. The grey one and small blue one of your kind took them away."

Good, Senraeni sighed. *Then can someone please explain what is going on, and what you are doing here? You are welcome here, of course, but your visit was a surprise to say the least. This contraption is remarkable,* he said as he looked over the ship. *Humans built this? I am sad to see that it is destroyed.*

***

"I can explain!" Eramine shouted and waved from the wall. "You need to get me to Senquena right away. She needs me to heal her!"

Who are you? Wait...Quena's hurt? Senraeni's face was one of panic as he flew the humans the short distance to the wall.

"As for you, brother of mine, you and True need to join the rest of the crew. Xolt will be back

178

soon, and you have to meet Jena!" Eramine said. "I'll explain the rest later!"

Where is Quena? Senraeni demanded as he lifted Eramine onto his back. *And how can you heal a Child of Earth better than she can heal herself?*

"Less questions, more flying!" Eramine snapped as she pointed to the shoreline she had seen Rulraeno swimming toward. "She's been poisoned with deypin, and I can save her."

Stars! Senraeni stumbled off the wall and took flight. *You can heal deypin? You must be Eramine, the miracle zarder that Amby's little one keeps mumbling about.*

"I'm Eramine, and you are the Leyrkan who is strangely aloof around his sister."

Senraeni was quiet for a few moments as he flew closer to the shoreline, and he squinted a little as if planning something. *Aloof?*

"Rulraeno seems convinced you don't love her and keep yourself aloof from her," Eramine explained.

Where did she get that idea? Senraeni frowned, before seemingly staring off at nothing. His face was stern and unmoving until the last moments, in which he suddenly had a grin as if someone had offered a particularly good piece of news.

"Honestly, are you in Leyrkan mode all the time?"

Leyrkan mode?

"You've been talking to other people, and maintaining the flow of conversation pretty well in spite of that," Eramine said. "I am impressed, but if

179

you're doing that around Rulraeno, you should know she's overly worried about what others think of her. She probably thinks you are deliberately ignoring her instead of trying to talk to everyone at once."

Stars, I don't mean to hurt anyone, Senaraeni sighed. *I have only been calling for help, and warning my joinmate not to come out here. The best healer I know, Telgrana, is coming here, and I am assured my beloved Grafi isn't going to risk hurting herself in the rain.*

"What was the grin for, then? That all sounds so formal."

Oh...that was a private message for a more proper time, Senraeni's cheeks had a redder hue to them.

Eramine laughed. "Okay then, I will just assume Grafi told you to hurry up and get back inside where it is safe."

Indeed, Senraeni said, his tone sounding unnaturally light. *But seriously, I don't mean to give the wrong impression. I love all my siblings. If I am in Leyrkan mode, as you call it, it is only to ensure everyone's happiness.*

"You should probably tell Rulraeno that," Eramine opined. "Look! There they are!"

***

Quena coughed deeply. *I am sorry, Rulrae. I...made you...dive.*

Don't apologize, my dear, Rulraeno said lightly, hoping that Quena did not hear the fear in her voice. *It was nothing. I would dive in harsher waters than these for you.*

And I...would not let you, Quena shuddered involuntarily. *My throat hurts...*

Rulraeno stared at the bleeding wounds in Quena's neck. If those arrows had been just a few inches lower...

Don't cry, Rulrae, Senquena said. *I am...fine. I just...need to...catch...my breath...*

We need to find Eramine, Rulraeno said as she performed the delicate balance of putting pressure on the wounds while giving Quena room to breathe. *She is going to use her medicine before we get someone to heal you.*

No need. I can...heal myself once I...catch my...breath.

You can, Rulraeno said. *But you are a hero of the Sandleyr now, my love. You get to relax now and let others do the work for you.*

Your...love? I didn't imagine it...you love me?

Of course I do, Rulraeno said, and it felt like each time she confessed it a great burden was cast aside. *Can you forgive me for ever denying it?*

Senquena smiled, and closed her eyes.

Oh no you don't, Rulraeno shrieked. *You don't get to give up like that. I can't face this place alone. Stay with me. Quena!* Rulraeno screamed, before frantically looking around the cove. *Eramine, where are you?*

"I am over here!" Eramine shouted as she ran to Senquena's side. If the girl was stunned by the wounds, she quickly hid her fears to start administering the healing herb. "She's going to be okay, Rulraeno. When Senquena was saving my brother, I found yours."

Which one?

The worried Leyrkan, Senraeni said, before pausing to stare at Senquena for an awkwardly long moment. Then he smiled and said, *She is hurt, but she is exhausted, not dying.*

Praise the Sky Lord, Rulraeno exclaimed, before she began to weep uncontrollably.

I have sent for my Telgrana, Senraeni said softly. *I found Senquena's parents as well. They are all coming shortly, once we've seen to the humans getting safely inside and situated.*

No! Rulraeno screamed. The memories from the flower field were still fresh. *Not them! Those monsters will make it worse!*

Telgrana is the best healer the Sandleyr has, Senraeni said firmly, anger filling his tone. *She has more than once proven her worth to the two kingdoms. Her advice once saved my life.*

Oh, I am not worried about her, Rulraeno said as she folded her wings closer to her side. *I fear the two monsters that somehow created a beautiful soul.*

Senraeni blinked as if stunned. *Senquena's parents are worried for her. I felt it.*

No, Rulraeno laughed harshly, *they are worried for him.*

Senraeni frowned. *What is that supposed to mean?*

Rulraeno stared at her brother for an awkward moment. Was it possible that the reason for Quena's torment was not known outside of the individuals involved? *You really don't know, do you?*

No, Senraeni sighed. *I have never claimed to know anything, especially when it is referred to in cryptic tones like that. I've grown to despise secrets and mysteries, especially when they burden those I care about.*

Senquena was found to be born Senkanna at birth, a pale green, elderly Child of Earth said as she landed nearby. After she quickly bowed to Senraeni, she added, *Her parents resent her for denying what they think is her real identity. I came as soon as I could, but I couldn't help but listen to their conversation after I heard them continuously calling her Senkanna and caterwauling as if they wanted the whole Sandleyr to hear how much they care. I hope you will agree with my decision afterward; I felt it best that I implied to them that she had been moved elsewhere, in the opposite direction from here.*

*I am not...Senkanna...*Senquena whimpered, though she did not open her eyes.

Of course not, my love, Rulraeno said as she gently stroked Senquena's back.

"Senquena was born Senquena," Eramine said to the newcomer, though she didn't look up until she was finished helping her friend. "Everyone else is confused."

Confused is correct, Senraeni said. *Telgrana, her heart and emotions are of a woman. How is it she was born Senkanna?*

The elderly Onizard frowned. *Shouldn't I be healing her wounds instead of worrying about irrelevant details about what others think of my patient?*

Thank you, Telgrana, Rulraeno shouted, her tone one of exasperation. *She may have been hit by deypin-laced arrows, but Eramine has applied the antidote just in case.*

The antidote? Telgrana turned paler as she stared at Eramine. *She has an antidote for deypin?*

Senraeni said nothing, but exchanged a look with Rulraeno that seemed as if he were experiencing the greatest of pain for the second time.

"It is common where I am from," Eramine said. "I am sorry that we didn't know you needed it here. I would have healed Ransenna had I known."

I would have loved to have it a few times in my life. My joinmate sacrificed everything in his search for the cure to that awful stuff, Telgrana sighed and bowed her head as if recalling a distant memory. Then, she got to the business of healing. *So she isn't feeling the effects of deypin. Why, then, is she still unconscious?*

She flew down to save one of the humans from that ship that's stuck on the rocks around the Sandleyr wall, and she nearly drowned after the arrows hit her and she fell into the water, Rulraeno explained. *She is probably exhausted. I know I am.*

She fell? Then how did she get to shore? Telgrana asked. *She couldn't have climbed onto the rocks. Her feet would have been lacerated if she tried. Stars, I'm surprised she didn't hurt herself tumbling into one of the rocks. She is remarkably lucky.*

I dove into the water, then I carried her to shore, Rulraeno said.

Both Senraeni and Telgrana stared at Rulraeno as if she had explained traveling to the stars and back.

You can swim? Senraeni asked softly.

Rulraeno started to blush. *That's not a big deal, I have been swimming every day for years. Besides, I would have gone after her even if I couldn't swim.*

Senraeni stared at her for a moment, then started laughing. *Well then, perhaps I will be performing a joinmating ceremony before long. Unless you want Mom to do it?*

That is Senquena's choice, Rulraeno said. *I know we both admitted our love for one another, but given this was in the middle of a crisis, I would rather tell her again when things are calmer so she doesn't think I told her out of duress or something.*

If you love her, you should tell her as often as you can, and in different ways, Senraeni advised.

I will, Rulraeno said. *I have denied it for too long. She could have died without knowing I love her, and I will never forgive myself for that.*

Believe it or not, I know the feeling, Senraeni said. *Not from my powers, I mean, I actually know the feeling from my own relationship.*

185

Eramine giggled, but went silent when everyone looked at her.

Also, for the record, Eramine explained a few things to me on the way over here, Senraeni said. *I may seem aloof, but I do love you the same as I love my other siblings. My Grafi teases me all the time for being bad at expressing my own feelings, even as I understand the feelings of everyone else. I feel awkward most of the time, but I will work harder on pushing through that, I promise.*

Rulraeno paused for a moment, then laughed. *Well, I guess we can't expect either of us to be good at social cues if we were both hidden away as children.*

Let's both agree to give each other another chance, Senraeni said as he held out his tail.

Agreed, Rulraeno nodded, before grabbing his tail and pulling him close for a hug.

She is healed, Telgrana interjected. *She is just going to need a little while longer to rest. I didn't detect any air in her lungs, so you must have gotten there before her head went below water, Rulraeno. That is impressive.*

She tried to swim like I do, Rulraeno said, a sense of awe in her tone. *I didn't know she watched me doing it before.*

"I could have told you that," Eramine shrugged. "Actually, I should have told you that. It might have given you courage."

She tried to swim while all those arrows were stuck in her neck? Telgrana shook her head. *You are both amazing women.*

"Speaking of how amazing the two of them are, there's one thing I don't understand," Eramine said. "Senraeni, when Senquena was having a panic attack, we all saw each other's memories when we touched each other. I was told only Children of Light could do that. Also, why did your mom try to recruit me as a matchmaker for those two? They didn't need my help, really. They just needed to tell the truth."

Senraeni and Telgrana shared a look of fear and worry. *What I am about to say does not leave this shoreline, understood?* Senraeni's voice was urgent.

"Ok," Eramine blinked. "Are they in danger?"

Maybe, Senraeni said. *There will always be those who desire power at the expense of others. The Day Kingdom is a powerful thing that has been fought for before.*

Rulraeno froze in shock. *Is Mom ok?*

She is fine, Senraeni said. *She was worried sick about you, and I guess that translated into powers coming early.*

I do not want to be the Heir of Day, Rulraeno said firmly.

You aren't, Senraeni said. *Senquena is.*

Rulraeno gasped and turned to her sleeping love. Then, after a moment's thought, she said, *That explains quite a few things. What must I do to help her?*

You will have to be there for her when the time does come, Senraeni said. *It is said a Child of Light without their true love cannot last for long, and I strongly believe that. Your love will help her more than you will ever know. But whatever you do, don't tell her what her destiny is.*

"Of course not, she would be nervous all the time!" Eramine said.

She deserves to have some peaceful time before she knows, Rulraeno agreed. *That is probably going to be our toughest day. I will have to grieve Mom and keep her grounded in love at the same time.*

Trust me, you will be able to do both, Senraeni said. *Just sensing that you grieve with her and are there for her will do more than most other things.*

Rulraeno blushed. *I will do my best. I think...perhaps it is time I had a long conversation with Dad and Mom.*

Senraeni smiled softly. *Tell them I said hello.*

The calm of the night shattered with several cries of *Senkanna!* Drifting into mind like a claw over slate rock. Senquena shuddered and moaned in her sleep, hiding her tail underneath her legs in what surely must have been a painful angle.

I am here, my love, Rulraeno said lightly. *The monsters won't get you. You will be safe, I swear on Cully's star.*

Rulrae, Senquena moaned. *You...really love me? It wasn't a dream?*

Of course, Quena, Rulraeno said. *I am going to keep telling and showing you until you believe me.*

Senquena smiled and relaxed slightly, though she still had her tail hidden as if it were a reflex.

Senraeni frowned. *I think someone had better explain what has been happening before her parent's arrive.*

"Of course!" Eramine said. "She told us her parents grabbed her and examined her after she hatched, then they told her she was Senkanna. They have been telling her awful things and doing worse things to her."

Grabbed her? Examined her? Telgrana said, her voice sounding as if she had scraped each word out of ice. The Child of Earth dug her claws into the ground. *A hatchling child?*

"They did worse to her," Eramine shuddered. "They are monsters."

Worse things? Senraeni said, his voice completely monotone. *What worse things than that?*

"You can see memories, right? Let me show you what I remember seeing when I saw her memory of the past."

Senraeni paused for a moment before he held up his tail. *No, I trust you to tell the truth. If you see my memory of seeing someone else's terrible memory, it will be a burden on you. Of the possible things you could see, most of them involve a gruesome murder or something I don't want others to see.*

"What is wrong with this place?" Eramine sighed.

I ask myself that often as I work to fix it, Senraeni said. *But tell me what you saw.*

Briefly, Eramine explained Dartenno and the torture beatings, as well as Senquena's fear she still had

189

for flowers. The more she spoke, the angrier Senraeni appeared.

They are lucky that I am Leyrkan now and have a kingdom's reputation to uphold, or else I might have made use of my training as a fighter, Senraeni scowled. *Rulraeno, do you want to tell them off or should I?*

Ideally, Quena would, Rulraeno said. *But as she is still sleeping, I will defer to you.*

Great, they found us, Telgrana frowned and stepped in front of Senquena as she stared at the two landing Onizards.

Where is my baby boy? Senquena's mother whined.

You do not have a baby boy, Senraeni said matter-of-factly. *As it turns out, I was mistaken in the severity of Senquena's injuries. You can go back to your leyr, as Telgrana has already healed her.*

Well, good that he's healed, Senquena's mother said, her voice lingering slightly too long on the wrong pronoun. *Can we see him?*

There is no him to see, besides myself, and you can see me perfectly well, Senraeni said in an eerily calm tone that didn't match his eyes.

Don't tell me you believe his perverted delusions of femininity, Senquena's father scoffed. *Next you'll start saying he's secretly a human.*

"What's wrong with being a human or a girl?" Eramine asked sharply.

Nothing, dear, if you are one, Senquena's mother giggled obnoxiously. *But you have to stick to*

190

the natural order of things. You can't be a girl just because you say you are one.

"I see," Eramine frowned. "If she says she is one, would you heal her if necessary, and treat her the same?"

I think we already know the answer to that one, Eramine, Rulraeno said with a pointed scowl at the offending Onizards. *They aren't worth the effort. I don't know how someone so beautiful came from such ugliness.*

I can't treat him the same if he is delusional, Senquena's father frowned back. *We only want him to be his true self. He is simply not a girl, and I can't help him if he insists on this falsehood in his mind.*

"Did you hear that, Leyrkan? They just admitted to being non-natured." Eramine said.

What? Senquena's mother shrieked. *Of course we aren't non-natured! Don't be ridiculous!*

"But they are!" Eramine shouted. "They swore an oath to heal without question or prejudices. I am pretty sure calling someone delusional and saying you'll treat them differently just because they tell you they are a girl is healing with prejudices."

Every Onizard in the clearing, with the exception of Senquena, stared at Eramine in awe. In the case of the offending Onizards, that awe seemed mixed in fear, as they lowered their wings and cowered. Rulraeno guffawed.

She is right, Senraeni said as he faced Senquena's parents with seemingly all the regal bearing he could muster. *I would strongly suggest you rethink*

191

your attitudes. If you leave my future sister-in-law alone without further foolish comments on what you believe is natural, I will ignore this transgression. However, if I hear you calling her by false pronouns again, there will be consequences. I can assure you, there will be no mercy in the Day Kingdom on this matter either, and they will be informed immediately.

Rulraeno is right, Leyrkan, Senquena said softly as she slowly opened her eyes and stood up. *They aren't worth it. I have struggled my whole life to accept that I was not good enough for them, when I should have accepted that they weren't good enough for me.*

How dare you insult us like that? We are your parents! her father snapped.

I am grateful for that, Senquena said. *But I can't be the Onizard you want me to be, and if you cannot accept that, we are better off being apart.*

Senquena's mother had the good sense to have eyes filled with tears. *Sweetheart, we just want you to be happy and normal.*

I am both, Senquena said. *So go back to the Sandleyr. Tell your friends I have survived, and I am feeling stronger than ever before. Acknowledge me as your daughter. Or do not. It does not matter what you say in the end. I have found solace at the end of a long journey and despite the odds, Rulraeno loves me too.*

Senquena's parents stared at her for a moment before grumpily walking back toward the Sandleyr.

Rulraeno folded her wings and bowed to Senquena. *I am sorry I lied about my feelings for you. I was afraid that who I am would hurt you somehow. I let the story of Ammasan and Senmani scare me into silence, when I should have realized that their silence was what doomed them to misery.*

There is nothing to forgive, for I had the same fears as you. Senquena said as she grasped Rulraeno's tail. *I swear to you that ours will not be another story like that. We will bring others into the light, and we will lead by example with love. We cannot go back to who we were, ashamed and alone.*

No, Rulraeno agreed. *I will not let fear and shame define me anymore. My heart is yours to share.*

Senquena smiled. *As is mine.*

Senraeni coughed and stared at the ground. *My offer stands to make the two of you joinmates when you are ready. It should be a lavish ceremony befitting two heroes of the Sandleyr.*

Oh, that wouldn't be necessary for us, Senquena laughed nervously.

"But you should let him," Eramine said. "If the story of Senmani and Ammasan is really the only famous story of same-gendered love your people have, there are bound to be others out there that are just as scared as the two of you were. No one deserves that."

You nearly died before I told you the truth, Rulraeno said softly. *If we can save someone else the pain...*

Of course, Senquena nodded. *Telgrana, do you think we could start planning a ceremony that spans both kingdoms?*

193

Telgrana smiled. *Of course. My daughter and son-in-law will love to hear about the water rescue, though they might teasingly try to compare who had to dive the furthest to come to the rescue of their love.*

"You mean this kind of thing has happened more than once?" Eramine shook her head. "I guess life is going to get far more interesting from now on."

Indeed, said a new, grey Onizard who was flying to join them on the beach. If he seemed to be looking around with his ears instead of his eyes, it was likely because his eyes were pure white and empty of anything that would help him see. What struck Eramine the most, though, was how much his jawline looked like Rulraeno's.

"You must be Cully's son," Eramine said. "I have heard a lot about you."

The grey Onizard landed and turned his head and ears in Eramine's direction. *Yes, I am Lord Iraeble, and you must be Eramine. I have heard a lot about you as well. You have been Invited, though we knew about this before the ceremony could even be official. I had hoped to find you in the Invitation Hall, but our family apparently does nothing by tradition. Anyway, it is time. The eggs are hatching.*

"If we aren't following tradition anyway, can Senquena and Rulraeno come?" Eramine asked. "I wouldn't be here if it wasn't for them, and they deserve a high honor for their bravery today."

Amby and I would be honored, Iraeble said, before he paused for a moment as if listening to someone only he could hear. *Oh dear stars, my children are rebels...Rulraeno, you should carry Eramine to the Leyr Grounds. Senquena, follow me. I am going to need your help.*

Does someone need healing? Senquena asked. *I will help if I can.*

No healing needed, but is an urgent matter, Iraeble said.

After a moment of seeming silence, Senquena gasped, then started giggling. *Go to the Leyr Grounds, Rulraeno,* she said as she and Iraeble took flight. *We'll be there shortly.*

"Well, that was odd," Eramine said. "What was that about?"

I am not sure, Senraeni said, *but I should be preparing a lavish welcome for the children and our new guests. Besides, poor Grafi will want to know what is going on. She's been stuck inside all alone this whole time.* With a bow, he took off for the Sandleyr as well.

Senquena must know who the other Invited is, Rulraeno said. *Why it was a secret is beyond me, though.*

"We'll know soon enough, I guess," Eramine said. She had a few ideas of who this Invited person was, but wasting time on guessing wasn't going to be productive when more important things were happening. "This fog and rain must be for the children. Do you think a worse storm is coming?"

Rulraeno laughed. *There are always worse storms, but we'll weather them. We should go. Your destiny awaits.*

"That sounds ominous and pretentious," Eramine said as she climbed up Rulraeno's tail. "Truth be told, I asked you to come with me because I am nervous."

That child knows you are smart, brave, and kind, Rulraeno said as she took flight. *She saw it from afar. Plus, you have already met in your dreams. You don't have anything to fear.*

"Yeah, well, there aren't exactly stories in my culture to prepare me for someone else being in my head all the time," Eramine sighed. "But I will do my best.

***

You have been Invited, Lord Iraeble said. *I apologize that I don't have time to explain what that means, but we must get you to the Leyr Grounds right away.*

"If you take one of us, you must take both of us," True said as she clung to Marinel. "I nearly lost him today, and I'm not going to be separated from him again."

"Our people need us," Marinel said. "Everything is confused. We've lost our home, our livelihood, and our futures. Now you're showing up saying that we have to come with you to some strange and unknown location when we should be helping everyone get organized and getting True a change of clothes. Besides, we still haven't found my sister, and that is the reason we are here in the first place!"

Iraeble's ears twitched. *Well, I don't have any intention of separating the pair of you. My children's hatching has already become some sort of a strange party, and one extra human isn't going to be a big deal. As for getting everyone organized, you can trust the humans and Onizards of the Sandleyr to help you in your time of need.*

Eramine is already up there where Lord Iraeble intends to take you, Senquena said softly as she landed nearby and tilted her head to look at True.

True gasped and stepped back.

It is okay, Senquena smiled. *I would have shot the arrow as well if I thought my Rulraeno was dying. I was frightened for a moment, but I truly am okay, and no lasting harm was done. You have incredibly good aim.*

Marinel raised his eyebrow. "Someone needs to explain to me later what happened while I was unconscious."

She was brave, and full of love, Senquena said. *She was willing to fight to the death to protect you, even when she thought you were dying. But none of that matters if we don't get the pair of you to the Leyr Grounds. You can climb onto my tail or Lord Iraeble's tail, but we must get you to Eramine and the others before it is too late.*

True hesitated, staring at the two Onizards.

"Go," a red-haired woman stepped forward from the mass of humans gathered behind the wall in a makeshift shelter. She smiled as she stared at True for a moment, as if in recognition of something, before handing her two new shirts, one just large enough for Marinel and the other in True's size. "I was afraid of the same thing once, but it will turn out okay. We'll talk later, and I will help you make sense of all of this."

"I haven't even found my father yet," True shuddered. "He was on the wreck with us, and I didn't see where he went."

"True!" Arvid called out as he rushed out of the mass of humans, his face pale as he stared at the blood that was still on True's clothing.

"I'm not hurt, Father," True said. "Neither is Marinel anymore. These creatures have remarkable powers."

The red-haired woman stared at Arvid and raised her hands to her mouth. Suddenly, True recognized how closely the two resembled one another.

Arvid looked up at the woman and nearly fell over. "Y-you're…"

"Dad?" the woman's eyes teared up.

"Jena!" Arvid pulled both of his daughters in for a giant hug. "You're alive! I don't believe it!"

"I don't believe it either," Jena sobbed.

"Where is your mother?" Arvid asked, his voice filled with hope.

Jena bowed her head. "She died a long time ago to save me."

"Oh," Arvid frowned and closed his eyes for a moment. "Well, I thought you were both dead when I set out on this journey. Having one of you alive is more joy than I could have ever hoped for."

"I've heard all about you," True said. "Father used to tell me about how smart and kind you were."

"Eramine told me a little about you before all this confusion happened," Jena said. "She said you were strong and beautiful. I don't doubt it now that I've met you."

Iraeble coughed loudly. *I love family reunions, but I'd love them more if I had some reassurance of my own child's safety.*

"True, I will watch over our father and your people while the two of you are up there," Jena said. "I promise a hot beverage, a happy family reunion, and an explanation of this place when you return."

True and Marinel took each other's hand as they stepped onto Senquena's tail.

***

"This had better be an incredibly powerful Child of Water hatching," Eramine mumbled as she shielded herself from the wind and rain by hiding between Rulraeno's legs. "This place has been inspected since you hatched, right?"

Of course, Rulraeno laughed. *None of us would have it any other way. Make sure you pay your respect to Lady Amblomni over there; she'll want to meet you, of course.*

"We already met," Eramine said as she waved to the dark Onizard with lavender eyes.

Lady Amblomni smiled and nodded her head in greeting.

I am not going to ever get used to the whole dream power thing, Rulraeno shook her head before

199

turning to the sky. *Oh look, they are returning with the other Invited!*

Eramine would have noted the new arrivals to the Leyr Grounds if she didn't feel compelled to watch the eggs hatch. The children almost seemed to be coordinating their arrival to the world, for as one claw would start to break through the shell, it would withdraw in favor of an eye peeking out of the gap toward the other egg.

Lady Amblomni seemed to notice this as well, for she chuckled and said, *Children, you can be whoever you want to be. Don't be afraid of one of you being the Heir of Senbralni. Just show the world what being the Heir means, and know that so many love you.*

The eggs rocked a final time, and the twins tumbled out onto the sand together in an excited flurry of squeaks.

Eramine watched the stormcloud grey hatchling to the left stand, and when the hatchling lifted her wings, it was a repeat of all the dreams she'd had before. Yet she wasn't afraid anymore; this was her friend stepping forth into the world, and as their minds connected Eramine felt none of the awkard feelings she feared would happen. Instead, it was as if a different part of her was awakening for the first time while at the same time she was reconnecting to a long-lost best friend. Perfect.

So I'm Amraeble by the way, her Bond said as she stumbled forward. Amraeble's brown eyes reflected both intelligence and the mischievous mood Eramine felt that her Bond was in. *I wasn't supposed to tell you until we Bonded for some reason. I can't wait until I can share the other secret!*

"Other secret?" Eramine blinked a few times, then turned her gaze toward the other hatchling, who was walking toward a familiar and unexpected pair. "True? Marinel?"

Marinel was trembling as he stood in front of his wife, arms outstretched as if shielding her from the Onizard child. True, on the other hand, was staring at Amraeble's twin as if she were confused about her own sanity.

To be fair, it was clear from the muscles on the baby, along with her fin-shaped tail and the sudden increase in precipitation, that the light blue hatchling was the powerful Child of Water Eramine had been merely joking about before. Also, Amraeble's twin did happen to have red eyes like the Fire Queen's eyes in the dream. But there was no malice in the child's eyes or body language, only shyness mixed with fear.

Oh no, Amraeble whimpered. *I hope they don't hate her. It'll ruin everything!*

"Ruin everything?"

We were supposed to each get a zarder, just like Mom, Amraeble sighed. *But the surprise is ruined now!*

Eramine gasped, then cupped her hands to get her message through the wind to her family. "Don't fight her!" Eramine shouted. "It'll be okay, I promise!"

Marinel frowned as he listened to the message, and he continued to stare fearfully at the child until True lifted her hand to his shoulder and kissed his

201

cheek. Then, to the surprise of everyone present, she bent down to the ground and held her arms open toward the hatchling Child of Water. The hatchling ran the remaining distance to practically launch herself into True's arms, and it was difficult to tell which one of them was sobbing the loudest.

"Of course I don't want to slay you! I don't deserve you, Ibralno," True said through tears. "I don't know what being a zarder means, but I know I saw you in my dreams, and now you're real, in my head, and we understand each other! I never thought I'd be raising a child again, but I'll do my best. You are so beautiful."

Being a zarder isn't about deserving things or having the answers, Ibralno piped up, her telepathic voice surprisingly elegant and full for a hatchling. *It's about having the most love. You'd cross oceans for it, you'd fight for it, and you'd die for it. You are my Bond, and when the time is right Marinel will understand. Until then, he loves you a lot, and maybe he'll learn to love me too.*

Marinel looked to True, then to Eramine, then back to True, before looking at Ibralno. "Look, I thought I was going to have to die to save True, and I made the sacrifice without question. I haven't understood anything that has been going on since I regained consciousness, but apparently True loves you like you are our child, so I will learn to figure it out."

We'd both die for True, Ibralno nodded and bowed her head. *But not today.*

Today, we celebrate! Amraeble grinned and flapped her wings.

Eramine stared at her family as they held an animated discussion with little Ibralno and Senquena. "Amrae, why didn't you just tell us from the start that True was going to be a zarder, too? Rulraeno and Senquena would have stayed and talked until True agreed to go with us."

It would have saved a lot of grief, Rulraeno agreed.

They'd have talked until True was as blue as my sister, and they still wouldn't have gotten her to go, Amraeble shrugged. *She had a zarder's heart, but she had to learn for herself that we aren't all like my ugly ancestor. Besides, if you both left, who would have been there to tell Marinel and the others how to find us?*

"That's fair," Eramine smiled. "Well, I'm glad we are all here together, and I'm glad I'm not the only new zarder trying to figure things out. There's only one thing left to do."

What's that? Amraeble tilted her head.

"We need to figure out if Marinel's going to Bond one of Amsaena's kids, or if he'll wait until Rulraeno and Senquena have babies. He lost his ship, so he's going to need something to keep himself busy apart from kissing his wife all the time."

Laughter, both human and Onizard, echoed through the Leyr Grounds.

The Ones in the Wilderness

Eramine is a fourteen year old who has just been told that she is destined to save a princess from certain death. However, the princess is not human, and Eramine's family is not convinced that saving the day is the right thing to do.

Rulraeno is a daughter of Rulsaesan and Deyraeno, which would technically make her a princess in Eramine's mind. A royal title is the farthest thing from her mind, however, since she has seen what has happened to those who have it. It would seem her only concern is protecting her young great-niece as well as her friend Senquena.

Senquena is a healer who specifically volunteered to help Rulraeno find Eramine. She is Rulraeno's closest friend, though she will dodge questions about the nature of their relationship if asked.

Marinel is Eramine's brother, and he has not taken kindly to two strange monsters taking his sister away. He has taken the family ship and his trusted crew into unknown waters to rescue his sister.

True is Marinel's newly wedded wife. Her mother died in the last attack on the village, and she is not going to let Eramine share that fate, no matter the cost.

Jamarius is Marinel's best friend as well as the ship's helmsman, and is active captain when Marinel needs him to be.

Arvid is True's father. A kind but brokenhearted man, he has had the unfortunate luck of losing two wives to the same murderous Onizard.

Hasana is the member of Marinel's crew who has the best eyesight, so she is more often than not spotted in the crow's nest.

Lord Idenno, Father Rain is a ghost Onizard who lives in the rainstorms and appears to those tied to the ancient bloodline of Senbralni. He can be a nuisance if he wants to be, though he generally only wants to be a nuisance if he thinks he can save people from danger.

The Fire Queen is dead, and no one has ever seen her ghost. Yet somehow her vile actions have impacted the lives of everyone in a negative way. While alive her "hobbies" included setting living things on fire and plotting stupid evil plans. Everyone is glad she's dead.

Inhabitants of the Sandleyr

The Day Kingdom

Leyrque Rulsaesan is the beloved ruler of the Day Kingdom, joinmate of Deyraeno and mother of five. She has outlived one of children and doesn't intend to let harm come to Eramine's Bond.

Deyraeno is the joinmate of Rulsaesan and the father of five children. He prefers avoiding attention when possible.

Lady Teltresan is the Day Kingdom's second Child of Light, joinmate of Delbralfi and mother of twin boys. She is a proud ally of the zarders and looks forward to eventually meeting Eramine.

Delbralfi is happy to let the rest of the Day Kingdom have all the attention, though he is a Lord on his own due to his connections with the Night Kingdom.

The Night Kingdom

Leyrkan Senraeni is a son of Rulsaesan and the Bond of Zarder Jena. His strong heart was tested by the tragedies that made him a Child of Light, but he finds comfort in his friends, family, and his beloved mate Delgrafi.

Lady Amblomni is the Heir of Senbralni, though she calls herself the daughter of Senraeni's brother Deldenno. Her children are destined to play a part in the Night Kingdom's history, provided Eramine arrives in time to properly Bond.

Iraeble is the mate of Lady Amblomni. He once let his physical blindness hold him back, but Amblomni talked sense into him after rescuing him from the clutches of the Fire Queen.

Jena is the first human to become the Bond of an Onizard, and also the first human to be the Bond of a Child of Light. Though she cannot feel Senrae's powers of empathy the way he can, she is a support system for him.

Bryn is the second Zarder, and the husband of Jena. No one can doubt his loyalty to his wife; he once travelled the wilderness to fight the Fire Queen on her behalf.

Delma found her way to the Sandleyr after the tragic destruction of her village when she was a ten year old child. As the Bond of Amblomni, she is currently the youngest Zarder at the age of 21.

Keegan is the eight year old son of Jena and Bryn. Doubtless he will be the next Zarder as soon as he grows to a sensible age for that type of emotional attachment.

Xoltorble is Bryn's Bond and the son of Teltresan and Delbralfi. He does not speak of the journey he took to fight the Fire Queen, as he feels guilt that he could not save everyone.

Delgrafi is the mate of Senraeni, though she still prefers to stay out of the spotlight if possible. She has proven to be a gentle-hearted Lady of the Night Kingdom and a great help to Senraeni.

Deldenno is a son of Rulsaesan and Deyraeno and Bond of Delbralfi, though he prefers to be remembered as a widower to Ransenna and a father to Amblomni and Randenno.

Telgrana is the mother of Teltresan. She acts as a messenger between the kingdoms, though she would refer to herself as the Night Kingdom's official healer.

Randenno is the son of Deldenno and Ransenna. His hatching was considered a miracle, since his mother died of deypin poison before his egg was fully formed. He dreams of doing more than guarding the Sandleyr from all dangers.

Ransenna was the joinmate of Deldenno, the Bond of Delculble, and the unlikely hero who saved Rulraeno from certain torture under the Fire Queen. Her murder haunts those who knew her.

Delculble, or "Cully" was Rulraeno's closest brother and the father of Iraeble. He died from the mental break that occurred upon his Bond Ransenna's death.

Sara Jo Easton drew the first Onizards when she was bored in math class (in her defense, it was the second day in a row of graphing a plane). Over a decade later, she has attended college for journalism and has travelled around the country gathering ideas for stories. Times have changed, but she would still get bored in a math class, especially if it involved two days in a row of graphing planes.

Contact the Author at:

Twitter: http://twitter.com/SaraJoEaston

Facebook:
http://facebook.com/AuthorSaraJoEaston

E-mail: zardermail@gmail.com